NIGHT
OF THE
SEVENTH
DREAM

LUCY LEWANDOWSKI

PARTRIDGE
A Penguin Random House Company

To order additional copies of this book, contact
Toll Free 800 101 2657 (Singapore)
Toll Free 1 800 81 7340 (Malaysia)
orders.singapore@partridgepublishing.com

www.partridgepublishing.com/singapore

This Book is Dedicated with Love and Thanks To

My Mom & Dad, Fay & Richard Lewandowski,

Eva 'Bim' Wood,

& Gaye Willox,

And all those who took me under their wing,

When I was featherless,

And my nest was fragile.

Lucy

Acknowledgements

Thank you to my daughter Rana Lewandowski for her cover and author photos as well as her encouragement to 'just get on with it already!'

To my son, Jai Lewandowski for his techno support and also to Sydney Felicio and staff at Trafford for patience as I navigate my way through the techno maze!

CHAPTER
ONE

The Day of the First Dream

The old lady ran her gnarled finger along the spines of the collection of books she had on the shelf. 'My word, this Bea Meadows was a prolific writer,' she muttered to herself. She'd had a good day, yet on this old timer's rollercoaster sometimes the good days were in fact the worst because it was then that she realised that so much of her life was now passing her by in the ever thickening fog of memory loss.

"Come now, Mrs. Morton, back to bed for you or your tootsies will get cold," said Nurse Laura as she bustled around organising the room with brusque efficiency for the night, then she softened and smiled at her and brushed back a glossy, black, curl that had escaped from her rather messy bun at the nape of her neck, no matter how hard she tried to look neat for work, she couldn't tame her mass of wild hair.

"I think I shall read this one, 'The Night of the Seventh Dream,'" she said as she drew out a worn book. Somewhere deep down in the recesses of her memory, she felt a hazy connection, this particular book tugged at her heart strings and she recalled it was her favourite.

"Well, I hardly think it matters, you've read them all a dozen times." Laura was tired and lacked her usual patience.

"Oh, have I, dear?" Mrs. Morton replied, puzzled.

"Do you want your feet done?" the nurse asked patting the faded patchwork bedspread, trying to compensate for her acid comment.

"Oh, that would be lovely, dear; it is one of my favourite things. Having my feet massaged as I'm filled with anticipation about to start a good book. You know I was probably a Japanese courtesan in a past life it so fills me with familiar memories."

The nurse vigorously rubbed some oil into the palms of her hands and started to massage the old lady's misshapen feet. "So, how are we this evening, Mrs. Morton?"

"We? Well, I guess I and the mouse in my dressing gown pocket are both well enough," she said patting the pocket of her well loved and faded velour dressing gown. "And how are you?"

"Yes, I'm well except that my body clock is all out of sync due to this run of night shifts, but I shouldn't complain, the pay is good."

"I remember vaguely as a young woman working some tremendously long hours, especially during the war."

"Somehow, I can't imagine you as a young woman," she replied tactlessly in her youthful arrogance, again allowing tiredness to taint her tongue.

"Oh, yes dear, we all start out young and grow old eventually; the trick is not to battle with it but to accept it gracefully. My, your hands are so warm with healing energy. You remind me of someone . . ."

The nurse busied herself around the room. She helped Mrs. Morton brush out her long grey scraggly hair. They had a very good reputation here at St. Francis' Nursing Home for giving that extra special touch. Indeed, this was why Jennifer Morton had chosen it for her mother when she had started to unexpectedly decline into senile dementia. Money wasn't really an issue, because she'd grown up with so little, when she had plenty later on, she'd carefully saved it for a rainy day. That day had arrived, and where nicer to be than in the care of attentive nurses in a home set amidst beautifully maintained parklands. After all, with a name like St. Francis', you couldn't really go wrong, anyone who could be kind to the animals had to be kind to elderly people, didn't they?

However, it was still an institution, if a somewhat deluxe one, and still ran to a time frame and budget, and the easy use of sedatives and sleeping pills, and mass produced institutional style meals. It was taxing work both physically and emotionally and the personal care assistants had a high turnover rate due to burn-out. Laura had been here for close to three years of dedication and was now suffering from frazzled nerves and dwindling patience levels.

Although the environment was considerately set out, Mrs. Morton still felt cooped up in her little room, it was compact but still charming and on her good days when her memory was sharp and clear she missed her home, her family, familiar things and her little garden of veggies and flowers. On these days she liked to sit in the courtyard and listen to the bubbling water in the fountain, she also found the comfort and companionship of a good book a welcome escape.

There was a tentative knock at the door. "Here's your supper and your pills, Mrs. Morton." It was discreetly left at the door so the nurse walked over and pulled the trolley close to the bed. "Take your pills then I can let you settle for the night." She said tenderly patting her shoulder.

Then Nurse Laura let herself out of the room, pulling the door ajar with a soft, "Have a good night, sleep well."

Her shoes squelched as she walked on the polished lino along the corridor to the staff room where she met up with a co-worker. They chatted amicably about the clothes in the latest fashion magazine which they flicked through and they also discussed plans for their days off and the needs and demands of their patients.

"So, what book did she choose, this time?" Her colleague, Kristy asked with a hint of cattiness in her curiosity.

"'The Night of the Seventh Dream,' it really is her favourite." Laura made a hasty cup of coffee and settled at the table to enjoy a piece of carrot cake and a brief break.

"Ok, that means we'll be on the 'Night of the Seventh Dream' roller-coaster for the next week. You know, I really think management ought to confiscate those books from her, they only upset her. Give her something less heavy, like Mills and Boon." Kristy absentmindedly twirled a strand of her fashionably multi-streaked hair in her finger.

"Well, the poor old biddy has had a hard life. Besides her daughter was firm, she wants us to provide her with as normal a life as possible, with plenty of pleasures. Just think it could be worse, she might have chosen, 'Seeds of Suspicion'!"

"Oh, yeah," snickered Kristy, the catty nurse as she pointed a perfectly manicured finger at a new season dress, with a handkerchief hem line and sporting a halter-neck, "Remember, last time, on the 'Seeds of Suspicion' rollercoaster, she lost so much weight because she thought we were trying to poison her, so she didn't eat. She pulled apart books, looking for love letters, checked our pockets for arsenic, and wouldn't take her pills 'cos she thought we would give her an overdose . . . . yeah, that one was bad."

"You know, I actually feel sorry for her, such a shame to lose your marbles at her age, 82 is relatively young these days. By all accounts and her daughter's description of her, she was a very intelligent woman." Laura said as she glanced at the fob watch on her ample bosom, noticing she'd spilt her coffee in her haste.

"Yes, I suppose but anyone who went through the deprivations of war, all that malnutrition, had to be affected." Kristy looked down to see how flat her stomach was this evening.

"I think when we got sick of hearing all the war stories over and over she lost some of her spark, she is quite sweet really." Laura rinsed her mug and dabbed at her uniform blouse then headed back to work.

Back in bed, Mrs. Morton had the delicious feeling of being snug and secure. Her teeth were frothing away merrily in the glass on the bedside table so she sucked on a square of Lindt chocolate that her daughter had brought in on her last visit. She felt peaceful as she wearily rested the heavy book on her tummy and started to read.

The barefoot orphan girl wandered along the cobblestone street. Her grey rags of clothes were thin and thread bare, no self respecting person would be seen in them, she felt ashamed and they were hardly enough to keep out the biting cold wind. She resignedly bobbed down to gather up abandoned food scraps and walnuts, which had fallen from a nearby tree. In one hand she held a puppet, she would sing and make up plays in the market place and passers-by would feel sorry for her and give her coins. The pennies were enough to just keep her alive. Today, no-one was about as it was a cold change. She huddled out of the wind, in the covered doorway of the local library, which was her idea of paradise, all those books, filled with other worlds to escape to. At the orphanage she had been a good reader in charge of teaching the little ones, before she was thrown out for inflaming the imaginations of the youngsters. She was half asleep when a foot nudged her awake. "What have we got here?" said a kindly couple all rugged up in their coats, hats and scarves. "Haven't you got a home?" the gentleman enquired. "No, I don't," she whispered back. "Well, then we better take you in, you'll catch your death of cold out here, come along," said the lady in a plum in your mouth sort of way. They gathered her up, took her home to their beautifully appointed house. As the Lady drew the young girl a bath, she explained that they hadn't been blessed with children and if the girl was well behaved she might be allowed to stay. Time passed and it was a joyful arrangement for all involved. They lavished beautiful clothes on her, gave her chocolates, and taught her to play the piano and even let her read from their vast, impressive library. She felt like their daughter . . .

"Beatty, time to get up." She woke with a start, dread and guilt filled her mind. "I feel like such a traitor," she thought, "I love my parents and they really do their best for me, for all of us, how could I betray their trust by having such a dream."

"Beatty, it is already 6am, your father needs to leave soon." Mother called softly from the kitchen, so as not to wake the younger children. Now that Beatty was fifteen she had a grey woollen blanket to form a partition in her room which she shared with Amelia who was twelve and going through an annoying busy-body stage and baby Evangeline most often called Evie who at one was the most cuddly, gorgeous, curly haired infant you could imagine, adored by all the family.

Beatty sat on the edge of her cast iron bed, trying not to make it squeak too much while she pulled on her thick woollen socks and then squeezed her dress over her nightgown which doubled as a petticoat.

In the kitchen, it was a bit warmer, the combustion stove was fired up and an aluminium pot of porridge bubbled away, with blobs escaping onto the stove top and burning, giving off curlicues of acrid smoke.

Although dingy, the kitchen was always warm and welcoming and usually smelt good. It really was the heart of the home; it was here that one kept a finger on the pulse of the life of the family. A colourful, home crafted, braided rag rug in its well worn glory graced the scrubbed wooden floor boards. Mother, a homely, pleasant looking woman in her late thirties was bustling around preparing breakfast, tea and a cut lunch all at the same time. She was the life blood, hard working and reliable, without her surely the family would perish, like letting the blood flow un-staunched from a major artery. Like all mothers, she wasn't truly appreciated. She was always up before Beatty, stoking the old Stanley stove, and she was the last to go to bed of an evening, Beatty didn't know where she got her reserves of energy from. Beatty turned the polished brass tap on the heavy cast-iron urn filling up the Fine Bone China Teapot, a well loved wedding present from Joyce's Mum all those years ago. It had fared well with only a few small chips on the spout, the springs of violets still looked fresh. The bergamot-y fragrance of Earl Grey filled the kitchen. Beatty tied the knitted tea cosy in place.

As she whirled around in her haste and reached over to serve the porridge she knocked the saucepan lid to the floor making a loud clattering racket.

"Clumsy girl, here give me that," Mother said elbowing her out of the way and grabbing the wooden spoon, "The last thing I need is for you to wake the baby, Gran and the boys. I've a pile of ironing to do when you and Dad are out of my hair." Usually good natured, Mother shocked Beatty with her uncharacteristic outburst.

Breakfast was a silent torture with Dad bent over trying to balance his books while eating his porridge and slurping his cup of tea. Mother seemed to be irritable and Beatty was still giving herself a hard time about her dream.

They carried the basket of sandwiches and biscuits out into the misty Melbourne morning to the Ford truck, her father's pride and joy and the reason behind the growing business. Beatty sat while her father cranked the beast over, then he hopped in, tucked a blanket about her legs, gave her a reassuring smile and said, "All set poppet? Don't worry about your Mother; she's got a bit of a bee in her bonnet because she's had a lot to worry about lately. We'll have a good day. First we have to swing by the honey factory to get a few things and I need a word with Bob."

"More like she'd had a swarm of bees, lately, but yes, we'll have a good day, I'm sure of it." Beatty enjoyed these trips to help out in the bush. Father rubbed his hands together both to warm them and out of excitement, his enthusiasm for bees was infectious and Beatty had caught the bug. Indeed Charles loved everything about bees.

He believed in the 'Rule of Three', that nearly everything to do with bees comes in three. Basically, there is a three year system to beekeeping, the first year in spring you buy a small colony, the second year they reach maturity and in the third year they will want to swarm and you will try to prevent it. There are three castes of bees, queen, worker and drones. The queen is really only a three year laying machine. It takes three days for the eggs to become a larva and soak up the food fed to it by the workers before it is decided if it will grow into a queen or a worker. Then, there are three main ways to obtain a swarm. Also, a beekeeper must wait three minutes for their smoker to be good and ready before smoking the hives when the bees will think that there is the threat of bushfire, gorge themselves on honey and go into a mellow soporific state. Yes, he could go on. He'd also noticed how things came in threes in his personal and family life, luck both good and bad often travelled in threes. Within three years of starting his business it was gaining a good income. His wife had an easy time giving birth to the first three but a hard time to the younger three, in fact the doctor had recommended that she shouldn't have any more babies. He also strongly believed in spring cleaning the hives. And the romantic in him loved the bee dances and cooperative structure within the hive community.

Even as a young man Beatty's father had always had a keen interest in bees, he read everything he could lay his hands on, this grew to keeping them as a hobby, then on to owning and using more hives, extracting the honey, storing it in tins then bottling it to sell locally and now an established business and running a factory with his best mate, Bob and Bob's nineteen year old son, Robin. He planned that when his own sons were old enough, to employ them, too, but in the meantime he had to be content with his eldest daughter, Beatty. He couldn't complain, she was strong for her age and a willing worker. Not a queen bee, this one, but a roll your sleeves up and buzz around busy, type of worker. Robin often accompanied him to tend to the hives but he enjoyed Beatty's easy good nature and quick wit. Robin was a solid worker but a serious lad. He mused about his own kids, Amelia at almost thirteen was a bit of a lady, and a lazy one at that, Harry at nine was a good boy if a bit spoilt being the first boy, the twins, Gregory and Rupert at six were a mischievous handful and the bane of his wife's life. And little Evie, his baby, well, she was just plain adorable with her dimpled smiles and warm milky cuddles. Yes, a large family was a blessing of his Catholic beliefs. Thank goodness, his wife's mother, Granny Florence also lived with them to help out with the chores. She was another mouth to feed, sure, but the scrawny old bird didn't eat that much, so, she was worth her weight in gold, that is when she wasn't crippled up and complaining with her arthritis.

The familiar fragrance of the air heavy with honey greeted them as they entered the factory. The converted warehouse was cool but had a drum heater in the corner to help the honey flow. The area was cavernous with heavy eucalyptus beams and within it they had built partitions, one for an office, another for storage of boxes. On these cold days they tended to gravitate to the heater for cup of tea breaks and to discuss business.

"Mornin, Bob and Robin, how goes it?" Beatty's Dad called out.

"Mornin, Charlie, Beatty," he nodded to her, "all's good, big order in from the grocer's in Sydney Town. Come warm yourselves by the fire, it's just starting to throw out some heat. It'll be a busy day to get it all packed and sent on time."

Beatty looked at Robin, gave him a shy smile then blushed beetroot red. Since the last time she saw him he seemed to have lost the gangly teenager look and now he was filled out she noticed he was quite handsome. Robin touched the brim off his cap and gave her a little nod, before continuing to stick labels onto assorted jars. It sure would be a good day when they could afford a labelling machine, he mused, but with the escalating insecurities of war that could be a long way off.

They chatted briefly, warming their hands by the heater, then Charlie grabbed a spare smoker and veil and they headed off to the hills.

"I'm a lucky man to have such a trustworthy partner in Bob, and that Robin sure is a well mannered lad, puts in a good day's work."

For a couple of hours the truck rumbled up the rough bush tracks, Beatty was lulled into a semi doze, she wished she could replay the dream and tell the well heeled couple she had a loving Mother and Father who provided well for her. She adored her Father and they both enjoyed the trip into the country to check the health of the hives and collect a small sample of the pre-spring honeycomb, only enough for a treat for the family, the main harvest wouldn't start for months yet. He didn't like the term, 'robbing the bees,' he preferred to think of it as, 'collecting the rent.' The bush opened up to clover rich pastures, here her Father had a deal with the farmer, who lived in Greendale that in exchange for honey he could keep his bees in this pure fresh corner of the country. On an isolated farm, bordered by the Lerderderg State Reserve the bees had access to pure fresh water and good clean pastures. Sure it was a big day trip to check on them but it was only every few weeks, the good thing about bees, Father always said, is that they practically keep themselves. The good thing about her Father was that he truly loved his bees, looked after them, and provided well for them and consequently them for him, he didn't merely keep them to exploit them. He aimed to one day own his own land for the bees, but it wouldn't be until after the war. He had a hunch that the demand and the price of honey would go up then.

They worked quietly alongside each other, smoking and checking all the hives to make sure they were healthy. They added on top boxes ready for the influx of spring nectar and honey production. They only stopped when it was too dark to see safely. "Well, it's beggared I am, Poppet, that was an 'onest day's work if ever I've worked one. Thanks for your help, love." He gave her shoulders a squeeze and Beatty lapped up the affection that she craved so much but had received less of as she became more womanly. Mother was not the demonstrative type, caring, considerate, thoughtful but not affectionate. They drove home in silence each absorbed in their own thoughts, looking forward to a roast dinner and pudding before bed.

Mrs. Morton slid the book under her pillow, switched off her light and lay there imagining things in the shadows on the wall. The light reflected off the water in the birdbath which was situated in the courtyard directly outside her room. Bees danced and flickered across the wall; the gentle breeze played with the gauzy curtains and brought the scent of jasmine and wafting memories which quivered at the edge of her consciousness into her nocturnal musings.

CHAPTER
TWO

Wrens in the Rain

Mrs. Morton woke with a start and the insistence of a brimming full to bursting bladder. As swiftly as her aching limbs would allow she made her way to her own cubicle en-suite, grateful that it was only a dozen shuffling steps away. With her morning ablution complete, she climbed back into bed to listen to the rain thrumming on the colourbond roof and waited for her morning cup of tea to be delivered. As she reached for a hankie under her pillow she came across her book. "Oh, that's right, I started this one, now where was I?" She decided she would feign illness to be allowed to stay snug in her bed all day, reading and enjoying the rain from the warmest place.

Beatty suddenly awoke with an urgency to visit the outhouse. She glanced up at the window pane above her head where frost glistened and crackled. Hastily she grabbed a shawl and wrapped it around herself as she made a dash to the dunny. Unfortunately, the door was shut and it was occupied, "Hurry up in there," she called out as she rapped on the wooden palings with her knuckles. She hopped about to her warm herself against the icy cold on the rough flagstone paths which lead through the garden, trying to avoid the fowl poop. The chickens were merrily scratching about in the dirt, seemingly oblivious to the penetrating cold.

"Drat Dad, why couldn't he have installed a proper flushing water closet as he promised," she grumbled as the frost licked about her ankles while she jigged in the garden. Father came out pulling up his braces and said, "And a good morning to you, too, Beatty Boo." She did a frantic survey of the wooden seat and surrounds for tarantula spiders, or a rogue red-back spider which might have spun a thread in anticipation of kamikaze swinging into her tender innocent derriere, all looked clear and in order so she sat down with a sigh of relief. She knew she wouldn't have long before the next family member needed to use it so she made a quick list of her chores and finished her business there.

The kitchen was humming with activity, today was Sunday and everyone was preparing for church. She loved the hive of activity atmosphere and the smell of freshly pressed Sunday best. "Pass me the candle stick mould behind you, Beatty, would you please?" Father asked. Today the sacred offering would be the candles poured last night from molten beeswax, just before he went to bed. "We all have to make ends meet in these times of strife." He explained. Beatty loved the pure wholesome smell of beeswax, it permeated her life, candles, furniture polish, shoe polish, soap, and skin care . . . to her it was the fresh spring air itself.

With the whole family dressed in their best clothes and bundled in homespun shawls they walked to the church. Father carried Evie who looked like an angel in her lace trimmed smocked dress. Because Gran had sore feet she decided it best to stay at home. Secretly, she liked the peace and quiet and the rare opportunity to have the house to herself. Church was a long painfully cold punishment and especially hard for the boys and Evie to sit still and endure the sermon. Beatty read the brass dedication plaques to help pass the time.

After the service, the cloying fragrance of incense wafted around as the grown-ups stood in the pale warmth of the late winter sun and caught up with the latest gossip. Usually, after the service they turned a blind eye to the youngsters running off a bit of steam on the other side of the cemetery, down by the banks of the slow moving river. The younger children were soon warm from playing tag in amongst the gravestones. Mrs. Richardson, the stern looking librarian with a severely neat bun and sombre clothes, came up to Beatty and said, "How old are you now, lass?" No 'hello,' or 'how do you do?', just straight down to business.

"I'm fifteen going on sixteen in less than a month's time, Mrs. Richardson."

"I've a job at the library going for a cleaner, would you be interested?"

"Yes I would be, but excuse me a moment, Mrs. Richardson, I'll ask my mother." Beatty went to search for her mother and found her in a heated discussion with one of the ladies, who had kindly offered her some second hand clothes for her family in perfectly good condition, but Beatty's mother insisted that they were not a charity case and could manage well without her 'help.' Beatty laid her hand on her mother's arm to get her attention, and then she leaned her head in and asked about the library cleaner's job in a quiet voice.

"You most certainly will not," she exploded, "No daughter of mine will be a cleaner, I have such hopes for you, with grades like yours you'll be a school teacher, tell Mrs. Richardson we'll not stoop to cleaning up after her learnered clientele." Beatty blushed from embarrassment and coyly went to tell the librarian the news, completely unnecessarily of course as she'd heard the outburst along with everyone else. The respective mothers called their broods of kids in to make a hasty departure. The boys came back, puffed and rosy cheeked but crabby that their game of tag was interrupted.

Lunch was usually a very special affair on a Sunday which was looked forward to all week, but today it was tainted with an awkward silence. After the dishes were washed and packed away everyone scattered in different directions. Beatty went to help her Dad in the backyard garden. The ground out the back attached to the narrow terrace house was also narrow and housed a tiny chicken coop as well as the outhouse, and a vegetable garden. They chatted amicably as they forked up carrots and turnips for the upcoming week, again her father made excuses for her mother's ever increasing crabbiness. The chooks gleefully peeked through the bucket of foods scraps in search of a tasty morsel.

"Yoo-hoo, I say Charles, are you there?" a voice called over the fence. A beaked nose popped over the fence and Mrs. Parker's face and tired washed out home perm followed. "Good looking carrots you got there, Charles."

"Good day, to you, Mrs. Parker, yes, they are a mighty fine crop, would you like some?" Charlie said as he tipped the brim of his old herringbone cap, and saluted with a bunch of earthy carrots.

"Oh, no dear I wouldn't dream of taking food out of the mouths of all your babes." She said as she adjusted her position on the wooden apple crate to have a better view of the garden. "I've a proposition for you, I have."

"And what might that be, Mrs. Parker?" Charlie said humouring her along.

"Well, with all your mouths to feed, and me with me bad back and now me two sons, Andy and Eddie, enlisted for the war effort, I thought you might like to work me back garden for veggies, too. You can hang a gate, turn the sod, plant it up and I can have a few veggies and your family can have the rest. Of course, don't tell your Missus that I'm helping you out, I know she can't stand charity, but you could say your helping me out 'cos me backs crook, what do you say?"

"Well, I say that is mighty kind and helpful of you, Mrs. Parker." Charlie took his cap off then squinted into the setting sun.

"Getting pretty brisk out, Poppet, what say we call it a day, not a word to your mother, reckon today isn't the best day to tell her." The house was warm and the scent of freshly baked bread was welcoming. Beatty's mother was humming a hymn as she organised the packed lunches for the next day. Charles washed up his hands then kissed her on her rosy cheek, "Feeling better are we Joyce, love?"

"Yes, I've caught up on all me chores. Thought I'd never get through 'em all. Beatty, give your Gran a foot massage she's been complaining about her rheumatism, says the colds creeping into her bones."

"Yes, Mum." Beatty ducked behind the blanket into the room which her Gran shared with Harry. Sat up in bed Gran knitted socks out of grey wool for the soldiers. Beatty rubbed her hands and massaged some life back into Gran's aching feet. "I'm not as young as I used to be Beatty, horrible thing this, getting old," she moaned.

"Come now, Gran, you'll only be sixty-nine in a few weeks. What'll we do this year to celebrate our birthdays?" Beatty chatted away trying to cheer her up, while giving her feet a vigorous rub.

"Well, I suppose love; it'll have to be a simple affair what with the rationing and all. No 'almost spring' trip to the beach this year. Still, we'll have some fun," she said with a twinkle in her eye.

After a simple dinner of leftovers from the roast, everyone sat around the wireless to listen to the latest news. Dad was one of a few scattered bands of radio home enthusiasts; initially he had a crystal set which he tinkered with while wearing bulky headphones, then he graduated from this primitive receiver joining a bigger wave of wireless fanatics and up scaled his set. It was still a big cumbersome thing made out of dark brown Bakelite and rigged up with an old gramophone speaker. He often walked around the little living room with his arm raised; antenna outstretched trying to get better reception. He was quite a whiz with tinkering that the General Electrics Company certainly didn't make much out of him.

They huddled together and craned to hear past the crackling reception of the radio. Finally, Father found some clarity. 'Good Evening, you are tuned to the Australian Broadcasting Commission for the Evening News Update . . .' As a treat on a Sunday they even got to listen to a comedy skit by Peter Finch called Dad and Dave. The needles clicked as the women knitted socks for the soldiers.

The squeaky wheels of the lunch trolley brought Mrs. Morton out of her reverie. The nurse on day shift helped to prop her up for lunch, "I suppose the vegetables are boiled to billyo, and tasteless is what they are. In my day . . . ." but the nurse had briskly continued on her rounds and Mrs. Morton was talking to thin air. She yawned and realised she was more sleepy than hungry so pushed the trolley aside.

When she woke she felt disoriented. She lifted the lid off the plate, lunch had gone cold. Without thinking she started to make a picture with the food from the plate, the chicken breast she placed in the centre on the pale velvet and silk bedspread, "That's the house," the beans she arranged to make trees, carefully she organised the corn kernels into rosettes, "Sunflowers, happy flowers." The carrot circles formed garden paths, windows, doors and a chimney. To make it look especially welcoming she smeared gravy out the chimney as smoke. When the picture was finished she rang the bedside buzzer for the nurse, so that she could help her get to the toilet without disturbing her work of art.

"Heaven's above, Mrs. Morton, what a mess, you're a silly sausage," the nurse exclaimed when she entered the room.

"Oh, am I dear? I thought it was rather pretty."

"Come now, let's get you cleaned up and sponge the mess off your bedspread so it doesn't stain."

She was helped into a fresh nightie and the bed was also made fresh. The nurse settled her in the armchair looking out into the courtyard.

"Sit tight, your daughter will be here soon, do you want a cup of tea?"

"Yes, that would be lovely, dear." She watched as the rain fell steadily, a family of blue wrens bopped about under the eaves, searching for bugs and worms. She'd always loved the blue wrens, they were her favourites. The biscuits with the tea tasted plain and uninteresting so she decided to give them to the birds, however, the window had a fly screen over it so without closing it again, she left the wind and rain blowing in, as she walked to the courtyard. The rain felt lovely on her arm as she threw out the crumbled biscuits, the earth felt good on her feet, so good that she ventured out further, guided by her own inner music she twirled and danced in the rain. Within a minute she was drenched, hair plastered to her head and her cotton nightie clinging transparently to her withered skin. This wild weather certainly made her feel alive. She laughed and tasted the rain. Under the overhang of the eaves she crouched down, huddling up with her arms hugging her knees to keep warm and watched the wrens foraging for their supper. Time stood still.

When Jennifer Morton tapped on her Mother's door which was ajar, she was shocked to feel the cold wind and see a puddle forming where rain was splattering in, the arm chair was empty. She looked in the toilet, "Mother, are you in there?" she called out. There was only silence as a reply.

She panicked then tucked her large shoulder bag under her arm, and jogged to find the nurses. "Do you know where Mother is?" No-one had seen her up and about. They raised the alarm; everyone was checking the dayroom, dining room and likely places, all to no avail. She walked with the lunch nurse who said, "She has had a bad day, today, she didn't get up out of bed or dressed all day, didn't know where she was, she didn't even eat lunch but made a big mess with it instead, so, don't expect too much of her when we find her. She can't have gone too far, not with our upgraded security system, so don't worry dear, we'll find her." The search continued with security staff called in and when they still hadn't located her, and the storm and night were rapidly approaching, the police were notified. "I don't see how she can have done a runner, she doesn't know the security code for the main door," said the nurse. Everyone was puzzled.

Luckily, the gardener spotted her as he collected up his abandoned tools for the day. "Come now, honey pie, what are you doing out in this? You'll catch your death of out here, let's go in and get you warm and dry." He said kindly as he offered his arm to help her up.

"Yes, it is getting rather cold and dark, I was feeding the birds. You know it's a long time since I was called 'honey pie.'"

Coming down the corridor, was a wet bedraggled old lady supported by a strong burly man. Jennifer jogged along, "Thank Goodness, Mother, where have you been, what can you have been thinking?" She blurted annoyed yet relieved.

"Actually, Jennifer, dear, I feel so much more alive now, he even called me 'honey pie'! I'll be right as the very rain itself after I have a hot shower and a dry nightie."

The nurse organised Mrs. Morton's shower and helped her back to bed while Jennifer wiped the armchair and the floor dry.

Jennifer looked at her mother and shook her head.

"Now, don't you dare tell me off dear, I feel so much brighter now. In fact, I actually feel glowing like that amazing sense of well being one gets after a day at the beach." Mrs. Morton explained to her daughter.

"But, Mother-honey, can't you do things which are less of a hassle in your quest to feel more alive?"

"You know, dear, I think I could have been a wild bohemian artist if my husband hadn't been so damn possessive. He expected so much of me yet didn't give me the space to be me and recharge, he really was a bastard but still I suppose it was wrong of me to do what I did to him."

"Yes, Mother, but what exactly are you talking about?" and rummaging around in her oversized bag she brought out a brown paper bag, "The usual installment of Lindt chocolate."

"Oh, goody, dark . . . that's my favourite, just what I feel like. I'll tell you the full story one day when you have time; I suppose I really should have a priest to absolve my sins before I die."

"Well, Mother you are incorrigible," Jennifer said keeping the topic safely on chocolate, "so it's easier to keep the peace by aiding and abetting your whims." No matter which variety she brought her Mother, she always said it was her favourite and just what she felt like.

"Oh, yes and here's your Dream Interpretation book, I borrowed." She said diving into the cavernous depths of her carry-all again.

"Oh, did you borrow it, I hadn't noticed. Good, you never know when I'll have a dream I might need to look up. By the way, when are the others coming to visit me? Perhaps you could even take me home for a day trip?"

"Oh, Mother we've been over this a dozen times, it only upsets them to see you like this."

"Like what? Oh well, perhaps one day they will regret it." Mrs. Morton resented the current society values of sticking old people away, out of sight out of mind, even from their own families who, she mused, really ought to know better. Time was when old people were considered a valuable resource.

"Well, I'm tired now after all this excitement so I might head home now."

"Ok, Jennifer, dear, I feel so bright now I think I'll eat chocolate and read all night, perhaps if I stay awake forever I won't sink into the dreaded la-la limbo-land fog ever again."

"Come now, Mother dear, be sensible, and read for a bit then rest. Sleep is good for you, too. See you in a few days." She leant down and kissed her forehead.

Mrs. Morton cracked the block of chocolate into bite size suck-able pieces, slid her book out from under her pillow and snuggled down to read.

She skimmed ahead to the next chapter.

CHAPTER
THREE

Birthday Blues

"Happy Birthday, dear Beatty," the family sang in the dark dingy house, made light only by the gaiety of the jovial atmosphere. Everyone had made such an effort to create a party, considering the war restrictions. Coupons had been saved for weeks to make a special meal. As Gran and Beatty's birthdays were only a few days apart they always celebrated together, but Gran preferred to have the focus shifted to Beatty as she didn't really like a fuss made of her, nor did she like a reminder of the rapidly passing years.

There was an unexpected rap at the front door, Charles walked along the narrow hall to answer it. "Ah, Robin lad, come in and join us, you're just in time."

"Congrats on your B-birthday, Beatty," Robin said and clumsily handed her a little gift, "It's not much."

Beatty blushed and bowed over the small parcel in her hand, concentrating hard to open it. This was the first gift she'd ever been given by someone outside the family, let alone someone of the opposite gender.

She took the lid off the tiny bottle of lavender perfume and had a tentative sniff, "It's beautiful, Robin, thank you so much," she said as she smiled up at him. Mother and Father exchanged approving glances at the well chosen gift and their shy demure daughter.

"Take a seat, son, plenty here to feed an army."

The twins, Gregory and Rupert emerged from behind the grey blanket curtain holding between them the handle of the picnic basket, in the bottom nestled a few parcels. As Beatty undid the worn wrapping papers, she found an assortment of presents, plain but practical socks knitted by Gran as well as a block of sweet smelling soap. There were drawings for her wall done by her younger siblings, and they had also put their pocket money together and bought a tin of chocolates, which of course they expected her to share. When she opened a rectangular shaped parcel she found a beautifully bound book with gold embossed writing, and complete with six coloured plates. It was in fact her all time favourite school book, 'The Secret Garden,' by Frances Eliza Hodgson Burnett. She ran her hand over the raised pattern and opened the cover; there written in her father's flourishing hand was a touching inscription:

To Our Dearest Beatrice, (15/8/1942)
May you enjoy creating your own secret garden,
Sweet Sixteen.
All our Love, Mum and Dad

She loved having her very own copy of this book; she threw her arms around her Mum and Dad in turn, thanking them. She ran her hand over her Dad's flamboyant writing, she loved the way he wrote his eights, her favourite number. Rupert pointed out there was still one gift remaining in the bottom of the basket and secretly this became the 'piece de resistance' present, it was a pair of highly desirable fine nylon stockings from her parents.

"We thought you would like a grown-up present for your sixteenth birthday, as well." They said smiling proudly.

"Yeah, sweet sixteen and never been kissed," teased her younger brothers but with a withering look from their mother they soon settled down and abandoned their taunting.

Beatty felt close to tears, she didn't feel she deserved all this attention and kindness. The dream still troubled her and not only that on her way home from school she had called into the library to see Mrs. Richardson about the cleaning job. She had thought about it for a month now, in fact she had thought of little else, she was sure she could juggle her schooling, home chores and a little cleaning at the library. She was relieved that Mrs. Richardson hadn't found anyone to fill the position yet. Only, she made her promise that her mother wasn't to know or to find out. She felt guilty going behind her back, but her instincts told her it was the right thing to do, and besides now she was sixteen, surely she had more say in her own life, not to mention increased responsibility.

"Smile, Beatty, move into the picture, Joyce," Father brought her out of her reverie by getting the precious box-brownie out of its leather case. Robin quietly rested his arm around her shoulders for the photograph. Everyone looked sombrely at the camera while the bright flash went off.

"If you want, Sir, I could take a likeness of you with the whole family," said Robin feeling more relaxed.

"Well, why not? It's not every day that your daughter turns sixteen. They swapped places and a well loved record of the day was taken.

Laura poked her head around the door, "You're still awake, Mrs. Morton, can I get you some sleeping pills."

"No, dear, I'm as content as a bee around a honey pot, it's so lovely and quiet here at night, gives me a good chance to wander in another world, if you know what I mean."

"Sure, I do, I enjoy a good book myself, buzz me if you want anything," she said pulling the door ajar.

"Hey, Laura, look at this, reckon we should put it up in the staff room, don't you?" giggled Kristy in the hall.

SUCCESS:

At age 4 success is . . . . . . not peeing in your pants.
At age 12 success is . . . . . . having friends.
At age 16 success is . . . . . . having a driver's license.
At age 20 success is . . . . . . going all the way.
At age 35 success is . . . . . . having money.
At age 50 success is . . . . . . having money.
At age 60 success is . . . . . . going all the way.
At age 70 success is . . . . . . having a driver's license.
At age 75 success is . . . . . . having friends.
At age 80 success is . . . . . . not peeing in your pants.

"Funny, isn't it?" Kristy asked.

"Yeah, I guess so, but you know we really shouldn't make fun of the old dears, before you know it we'll be old, too." Laura said.

"Oh, lighten up, Laura; you're getting too serious in your old age, it must be about time for you to have a break from here." Kristy flicked her hair and spun on her heel to continue her rounds.

Mrs. Morton listened to the hushed exchange in the corridor; she too could remember a time when getting old was inconceivable. 'Now where was I, before I was so rudely interrupted?'

"Dad, did you get the letter on the hall table that came today?" Harry was in charge of the meager in-coming and out-going mail. "No, son, I haven't seen it yet, bring it to me, will you?"

Charles torn open the letter, his face blanched ghostly pale. "Why, what is it Charles?" asked Joyce concerned by her husband's pallor.

"Well, I hate to spoil Beatty and Gran's party, but me numbers come up, I'm being called away to help fight the bloody Japs." He explained.

An uncomfortable silence descended. Robin bravely broke it, "Ack, ack, actually, sir, my D-dad wants a word with you about the f-f-actory." Robin stuttered.

"Don't say he's been called up, too. That'll be the ruination of the business." Charles said, colour rushing back into his face.

"I-I-I've been called up, but Dad won't let me go, he says it'll break Mum's heart, he'd rather go and leave me to run the factory." Robin said.

"Well, excuse me ladies, sorry Beatty and Flo for spoilin your do, but I better go around to Bob's for a pint. I'll have to take Beatty and Robin to the bees to show them what to do, while I'm away. Beatty, say good-bye to your guest." He pushed back from the table, adjusted his braces and then bounded up the narrow stairs to the little room which he shared with his wife, next to a tinier room which the twins shared; he grabbed his coat and scarf.

Meanwhile, Beatty walked Robin to the door. Feeling a momentary burst of confidence now they were alone, he gave her a quick kiss on the lips. Beatty was taken aback. "I just wanted to remedy what your brothers were saying." Robin explained. "Hope you won't hold it against me that I wanted to steal a kiss from you."

Beatty with her cheeks flared red and her lips on fire rushed to fling herself down on her bed and process her day. Amelia came to see what was wrong. "Leave me alone, 'Melia, go away, I just want to be alone."

"Amelia, leave her alone, she's had a big day, she's just upset about Dad, come and help me clear up in the kitchen." Thankfully her mother called. There was so much to be upset about, her dishonesty, her interrupted birthday, Dad being called away to war and now Robin's kiss. Evie crawled under the blanket partition and toddled beside her bed; Beatty scooped up her warm, cuddly body, buried her head in her tummy and sobbed. Evie plastered her with sloppy kisses and gave her "Der, Der," pats on the head with her warm sticky hands.

The next morning, Beatty woke up, got up and dressed before her mother called her.

"Mornin, Mum." She said as she walked into the kitchen.

"You're up early, dear." Her mother replied.

"Mum, with my school teaching entrance examinations coming up soon, I have to go in early and stay back a bit later; I've fallen a bit behind lately. Amelia can help get the boys ready and walk them to school, it's about time she did a bit more to help out, anyway."

"I suppose so, dear, but make sure you are home before dark." She hurriedly made her lunch then handed Beatty a brown paper bag with a baloney sandwich and honey oat biscuit and gave her a rare warm kiss on the cheek. Beatty fleetingly thought of Robin's kiss and blushed. These days the blood never felt far from the surface of her skin.

Pulling the shawl around her head she walked briskly to meet Mrs. Richardson at the library. Usually, Mrs. Richardson preferred to employ the services of a young man as janitor to keep her beloved library clean. With so many of the young men called away she'd had difficulty filling the job, whisking around herself before going home to tend to her four children. Before her good for nothing husband had been called away to war, he'd been laid off his work, and gotten stuck into the grog, forcing her to get the job as librarian. Previously, before she'd had her brood she'd been a school teacher, so supervising in a library wasn't so very different. What surprised her was the incredible sense of self worth she had gained by it, no longer only being the downtrodden wife of a drunken slob, but being Mrs. Richardson, the librarian. Now she felt she was a remarkable respected pillar of society.

Beatty knocked on the door and Mrs. Richardson let her in with a nod. The cold was worse inside than out, and a still frigidity crept into her bones.

Mrs. Richardson showed her to the cleaning supplies stored in the walk-in closet and demonstrated the level of cleaning standard she expected. Beatty could tell she would be a hard task master.

Battling her chattering teeth, Beatty asked questions about her times.

"Dust in the morning, do the black-wood counter and table tops and chairs, then do the floors and lavatory after school. Oh, yes, and you'll want to get hold of some of your Dad's thermal long johns, we never heat in here after hours." Mrs. Richardson showed her the cloths she'd need. Under her watchful eye, Beatty dusted down the books and polished the solid tables and counter until they shone to a mirror finish.

"Time for you to get to school, here's a key, never give it to anyone, I'm trusting you to be honourable." Mrs. Richardson handed her a heavy brass key on a long loop of ribbon so she could wear it around her neck hidden under her dress.

After school Beatty hurried to the library to sweep, mop then polish the floor boards. In the lavatory she took especial care to make the brass fittings on the wooden toilet seat and the curved taps and spout, gleaming. She wiped the porcelain hand basin til it was pristine. Secretly she wished they had a toilet and porcelain hand-basin to polish at home. She was quite tired by the time she got home but of course couldn't let on so she resignedly helped clean and chop the vegetables for the stew.

When the stew was bubbling merrily on the combustion stove, Beatty planned to have a sit down and cup of tea but mother said, "Beatty, I'm behind with the laundry, could you do the wringing?"

Beatty wearily made her way to the lean-to wash room at the back of the house and started pushing the boy's overalls through the mangle. As she cranked the stiff handle she thought of how much was required of her because she was a willing worker and how much her siblings got away with because it was such an effort to get them to help out.

As she wrung the water out of the clothes she felt like she was wringing out the last drops of her energy, how could she ever keep up this pace? Tears welled in her eyes, they ran down her cheeks and it wasn't long before the front of her apron was as wet as the washing she was wringing. She knew it was just weariness making her overcome with emotion so she hastily wiped her tears on the bottom corner of her apron and mentally told herself to pull it together.

CHAPTER
FOUR

Useless Dreams

"Beatty, I want a word with you when you're ready for school," her mother said when she walked through the kitchen on her way back from the out-house.

"Yes, Mum, I won't be long," Beatty replied. She hastily got dressed worried she was in some sort of strife and aware she didn't have long before she had to be at the library.

They sat together at the well worn, heavily scrubbed table, warming their hands against the cool morning air with their cups of tea.

"You may as well know, dear, since your father is away, that I am expecting. I'm about six weeks along."

Beatty frowned, puzzled then blushed vividly, having learned recently from a reference book at the library how babies are made. This job was really proving to be an accelerated education. She felt flustered to think of her parents that way. In another way she felt relieved that it wasn't her in trouble but now she felt burdened with her Mother's trouble.

"Does Dad know?" She asked.

"No, it must have happened just before he left, I didn't know for sure myself, but now I'm certain, I'll probably write to him." She said, "Actually, had I known I probably wouldn't have told him anyway as I know how important it is for him to defend his country."

Beatty was shocked; she looked closely at her mother for the first time in weeks. She'd been so caught up in her own affairs and general misery she hadn't been paying enough attention to those around her.

"Don't worry Beatty, dear, it'll be alright, I've had six healthy babies already, this way I can keep a bit of Daddy inside me while he is away and surprise him with it when he gets back."

"Have you been well?" Beatty asked suddenly overwhelmed with guilt.

"Yes, fine, I'm passed the worst of it. Stop fretting and don't say anything to anyone, this is our own little secret between you and I and Gran, for now, understand? I don't want the little ones spreading stories or I might end up with triplets, you know how they are."

"Of course, Mum, I better go now, lots of study to do. I'm behind in my French class. Au revoir, Cherie." Beatty grabbed her lunch, gave her Mother a quick kiss on the cheek and fled down the hallway.

"Don't be so late getting back, as the pregnancy progresses I'll need more help around home." Mother called after her.

Beatty's head was in a spin as she hurried down the street, recklessly dashing across the roads without checking. Automatically, she tugged at the brass key, and heard the familiar reassuring clonk as it turned in the lock. Used to the familiar morning routine she grabbed her dusting cloths and got down to work. Beatty loved the early quiet at the library; this morning in particular she had a lot to process. She found herself working robotically while fantasy scenarios played out in her vivid imagination.

While she was vigorously dusting, a book fell with a clatter to the floor, arousing her from her daydream. It was H. G. Well's 'A Modern Utopia,' fallen open to page 342. The lines, 'Scars of the past! Scars of the past! These fanciful, useless dreams!' leapt out from the page. She was jolted alert, hastily glancing over her shoulder to make sure Mrs. Richardson hadn't arrived yet. 'Scars of the past! Useless dreams! Whatever can this mean? Maybe it is a sign.' She muttered, still haunted by the orphan child dream.

She carefully checked that the little book wasn't damaged. She smelt the leather cover and ran her hands over the raised gold embossing. Apart from the incredible escape into the written worlds within books, Beatty just simply loved books. Their different shapes and sizes, their smell, linen or leather bound, a book was a treasure to behold. Working in the library was a blessing and a joy for Beatty, she took such pride in dusting, straightening and neatening up the books that to her even cleaning there was a pleasure. She pushed the book back on the shelf between 'War of the Worlds' and 'The Time Machine' aware that this author wrote outlandishly weird science fiction and that it didn't have anything to do with her meandering mind.

That afternoon, Robin who had been keeping an eye on Beatty so that he knew her general movements, sat on the cold concrete steps waiting for her to knock off.

When Beatty pulled the door closed and turned the stiff lock, she noticed Robin and flew into a rage, "How dare you spy on me and follow me around." She fled down the steps, and walked briskly in a huff, Robin jogged to catch up. Actually, she was more concerned that her Mother would find out about the job, take away her purpose and also the pleasure she derived from adding her contribution to the housekeeping tin in the corner of the kitchen cupboard. She knew her

Mother was puzzled by the seemingly unending surprise money but as yet she had said nothing.

"Beatty, don't be as angry as a hornet, if your Mother doesn't know, you can be sure I won't let on." Robin assured her. "Here, let me carry your school satchel, and you can tell me all about it."

They walked companionably along and Beatty was able to share her library experiences with someone for the first time. She felt slightly embarrassed by the animation with which she told him about her cleaning job.

Mother invited Robin in for a cup of tea and Beatty shivered involuntarily as they entered the dim, cool interior of the terrace house she called home.

The little children jumped and tugged at Robin's sleeve, they were so hungry for some male attention. "Come and play marbles with me?" pestered Harry.

"Not now lad, I've to talk to the ladies." He replied.

"Scoot, children, go out and play." Mother grabbed her apron and started to prepare afternoon tea.

Gran bustled in with a wicker basket piled high with washing balanced on her hip. She set in down and sank onto a wooden kitchen chair with a sigh.

Mother leant across the table with a plate of biscuits, "Would you like one of my honey oat biscuits?"

"Would I ever, you make the best honey oat bikkies, Mrs Fie . . ."

She abruptly cut him off, "Come now, Robin, call me Joyce, we see enough of you these days and now you have so much responsibility at the factory, it's only right."

"Thank you, Joyce," he nodded.

"You know, when our Beatty was only six, she squirreled some of these bikkies away in a jar. I had the date written on the label. A year later when I was cleaning out under her bed, I found them. They were as fresh as the day I baked them, according to Charles, so they do keep well, too. I made her eat one also, as a lesson not to hide food or waste it, but it wasn't really a punishment at all. Was it Beatty?" Mother enjoyed telling stories of the funny things her offspring had gotten up to.

"Well, in that case, when I get called up, I'll have to get you to make me some to take with me to remind me of home. They call them 'Anzacs' in the army, I've heard." Robin reached for another, not realising that he had created an awkward silence.

'Drat,' Beatty thought, 'why am I surrounded by men filled with pride about defending their country?'

"But I thought your father, Bob went to save you so you could run the factory, you won't get called up, surely?" Mother asked.

"No, probably not, but I-I-I do need a word with you about that, the business, I mean." Robin shuffled in his seat. The added responsibility at the factory had done him a power of good and his newly acquired self confidence had all but erased his stutter.

"What's wrong?" Mother's brow furrowed.

"Nothing really, but I need a hand to move the bee boxes, and to catch up in the factory, I'm awfully behind on my own. I thought Beatty could help me out on the weekend, maybe?"

"Absolutely not, I've seen the way you look at our Beatty." Mother exploded.

"Joyce," Granny Flo said soothingly, "Be practical, Harry could go too as a chaperone and an extra pair of hands, it wouldn't hurt him to help out a bit more. Amelia could go, too, let the little lady do some real work for a change."

"Well, I suppose so, come bright and early on Saturday with the Ford, and make sure you have plenty of fuel and check the water, I'll pack the four of you some lunch." Mother acquiesced.

"But, you make sure you treat her like a lady, lad or I'll skin your hide," Granny chipped in.

"Certainly, I will, see you at 7am, Beatty, thanks for afternoon tea, Joyce." Robin left, stumbling over a marble abandoned on the path.

"I expect you to remember your good Catholic values, child. Seems to me he's set his cap for you."

"Yes, Mother, I will." Beatty agreed.

That night while Mother and Gran twiddled the oscillator knob on the radio and waved the antenna around to get good reception to tune into 'The Radio Doctor' giving advice on health and fitness, Beatty invited her young siblings onto her bed to listen to 'A Secret Garden.' In a flourish of generosity she handed around the last of her birthday chocolates. With gobs stoppered with sweet goo, and crocheted rugs wrapped around their shoulders, she read to them fluently and with mesmerising intonation. The children particularly liked it when she tried out the Yorkshire accent of Ben Weather-staff, the gardener. They all became engrossed in the story, with the exception of baby Evie who was lulled to sleep. Beatty was pleased she could make the evening easier for the two older women who longed to put up their feet by this hour, and rest while knitting. They were making many pairs of socks to donate to the soldiers but Beatty was a slow knitter and besides she hated knitting socks so she was still on her first pair.

She briefly joined the women after reading and said, "Gran, while I'm at work . . . 'she shook her head' . . . I mean school tomorrow can you please turn the heel on my dratted sock?"

"Beatty!" Mother's look cautioned her on her choice of language.

"Sure, dear, you've been so busy lately."

"You know Beatty, sweetie, we really do 'preciate all your help." This was high praise coming from Mother who rarely complimented anyone.

Saturday couldn't come fast enough for Beatty who looked forward to spending the day with Robin even if it was for all intents and purposes, to work. She woke early and helped to prepare the picnic lunch, lugging the basket to wait by the door for Robin's softly considerate knock. Harry was a bit begrudging as he wasn't used to having to be up and out by seven and Amelia kicked up such a fuss that Mother let her off the hook out of sheer exhaustion and of course Mother insisted on a decent breaky of porridge.

The drive was quiet and uneventful; it was hard to talk over the noise of the motor and the rattling and squeaking caused by the rough roads. Beatty sat on the other side of Harry who was in the middle, occasionally Robin glanced at her and they exchanged shy smiles.

When they arrived they donned the white protective overalls, the wide brimmed hats with wire veils attached and the gloves to protect them from bee stings. Firstly, the bees had to be sedated by some smoke, then a small quantity of honey and honey comb harvested to make the boxes more manageable before tying the individual units together so that they could be lifted onto the back of the ford flat-tray truck and moved to their new clover pastures for spring and summer. It was hard and heavy work. Usually it was wiser to move the boxes at night but with the distance to travel they had to take the risk by using copious amounts of sedating smoke.

They found a sheltered spot to place the bee boxes, nestled under some eucalyptus trees. A chill ran down Beatty's spine, she sensed someone watching her, she hastily looked around but apart from the wind rustling in the leaves there was no sound or movement, "Are you sure this is where Dad said to put the hives for summer?" she asked Robin. "Well, I think so; he told me so much in the last few days before he left. It'll have to do, we've already moved half."

They drove back to the remaining boxes for lunch, Beatty spread out a chequered picnic rug on the lush cushioned grass and they ate their sandwiches and drank tea made hot from the thermos. Harry wasn't a very diligent chaperone and he wandered off to play branch boats in the nearby creek. Beatty lay down to rest briefly before they had to get back to work. Robin shuffled himself to rest alongside her, raised on an elbow, looking down at Beatty. He leant down and kissed her. Despite all the well intentioned parental warnings Beatty didn't protest because she found the tugging sensation within too enjoyable, surely something that felt this good couldn't be all that bad! Robin held her to him and stroked her through her clothing. He ran his hand up her woollen stocking clad thighs. Their breathing quickened. The petting got heavier. Just when they were precariously close to the point of no return . . . . Mrs. Morton put down her heavy book and stroked herself, enjoying the pleasure it brought. The chapter had brought back the sexual aliveness of her youth. She had a private giggle when she thought of the horror the young nurses would be in if they knew. She still felt young although her skin was aged and wrinkled. Why shouldn't she derive pleasure from her body? She dipped her fingers into her honey sweet nectar centre and let out a gentle sigh. She squeezed her legs together and continued reading . . . . all of a sudden a voice interrupted, "I guess this is what Mother told me I should tell her about." Harry stood over them mockingly. Beatty hastily pushed down her skirts and grabbed a biscuit to throw at him. Robin ran after him, wrestling him to the ground playfully and sitting on him until he swore secrecy.

They drove to the new place and set up the wooden hives in silence, adding additional super boxes for the summer harvest. They just finished as the shadows started to lengthen and the cold dew was settling. On the way home Harry fell asleep and Beatty protectively

37

put her arm around him, cradling his head against the bumpy road on her soft bosom. Fervent glances and smiles were exchanged. "You may as well know, Honey Bee, I'm mighty fond of you," Robin said softly so as not to disturb Harry.

When he dropped them off he thanked Joyce and said they'd had a wonderfully successful day, but they weren't finished and would it be possible for them to come to the factory after church for a few hours to help with a relatively large order. She supposed it was.

Beatty woke early again filled with anticipation. She dressed in her Sunday best and admired her slim shapely calves as she straightened the black seam on her new nylon stockings. After church she'd help Robin at the honey factory and hopefully Harry would lapse in his vigil, escaping to play with his marbles, allowing them another stolen kiss.

On Monday, Beatty momentarily sank into the librarian's padded velvet chair exhausted from her hectic schedule, and the heavy work on the weekend, she'd also had a big day at school and wondered how long she'd be able to keep up this rigorous routine. Before she knew it, she had dozed off.

A buzzing filled her ears, the market is a noisy colourful place filled with life and music. She sees herself sitting on a low bench dressed in scanty seductive clothes. On her lap she nurses a lamb. Nearby a clown wearing a 'Pierre poi-rot' happy/sad mask, is juggling apples. He tempts her with one, as she puts her hand out to accept it; it turns into a leather bound book. She runs her hand over the raised embossing on the cover, the book is called, 'The Golden Madonna.' She looks in the inside cover, her name and appreciation are on a gold embossed certificate. Before her eyes, the book disintegrates and she is holding a pile of dust.

Suddenly Beatty woke with a start. She could feel a painful crick in her neck from the awkward position she'd fallen asleep in. The cold had seeped into her damp clothes. She shuddered and feeling guilty hastily finished off her afternoon work, tidying up her supplies conscious of the lengthening shadows and the fact that Mother would be expecting her to help get the children their dinner and get them ready for bed. Also, Gran loved a foot massage of an evening.

She was just starting to feel sorry for herself when she noticed Robin in the Ford out front; he called out, "Hey, Honey Bee, thought I'd missed you. Figured you would 'preciate a lift home."

"Oh, Robin, you are sweet and I sure would, I fell asleep at work just now, hope Mrs. Richardson doesn't notice I didn't do as thorough a job as usual."

Beatty was troubled by the dream, what could it possibly mean? Was the dream telling her that her life would collapse into a pile of dust? Robin stole a kiss as he dropped Beatty off. Feeling flustered and with flaming red cheeks, Beatty quietly let herself in and sank on her bed, drawing out her glass rosary beads from under her pillow. She muttered, "Hail Mary, full of Grace, absolve me of my sins, oh blow the formalities, Dear Mary, Mother of Jesus, forgive my dreams, bless me for I know not what I dream." Sixteen was proving to be an enormously confusing time, confusing dreams, confusing sexual awakening, such a muddle. She missed her Father terribly, tears welled in her eyes and ran down her cheeks, and before she knew it she was asleep through utter exhaustion.

Mrs. Morton reached under her pillow for another piece of chocolate, to her disappointment she found she'd finished it off. Running a finger over the foil to collect up the crumbs she sucked them off, savouring the last sweetness. She flicked off the light. The moon shone in, light reflected off the water in the birdbath, throwing dancing creatures on the wall. 'Hang on a moment,' she thought feeling an overwhelming sense of déjà vu, searching in the archives of her mind for the familiar missing puzzle piece. She slipped out of bed, her feet touching the cold tiles and she wandered out. Looking down the corridor, vaguely aware of what she was searching for, she wandered along. She pushed at the door leading onto the courtyard, the air was brisk and she drew it in sharply. The moon light bathed the area in an ethereal light, she gasped at the violet light, it was breathtakingly beautiful. Spontaneously, she started to sing, "I'd like to teach the world to sing in perfect harmony, grow apple trees and honey bees and snow white turtle doves . . . ."

Suddenly, the door burst open, "Mrs. Morton, what in the world are you doing out here, you'll wake everyone up, howling at the moon," Nurse Laura firmly grasped her arm, "come, back to bed for you."

"Goodnight, smiling moon," Mrs. Morton whispered.

Back in bed Laura insisted she take a sleeping pill.

Kristy poked her head around the door, "Looking for the hereafter again were we, Mrs. Morton?" Kristy smirked, "What the heck were we here after?" Kristy had a giggle at her own joke. "Need me for anything, Laura?"

"No, Krist, I've got it under control."

Laura tucked the sleepy old lady in, drawing up the once luxurious bedspread, now showing signs of advanced age and wear, impulsively she kissed her crêpe cheek. She was fond of this one's wild passion, which most of the other nurses viewed as a dashed nuisance.

CHAPTER FIVE

Paper Elf

The next morning when Mrs. Morton awoke, she felt like she had a hangover, not that she'd ever really had one, but she imagined it felt like this. Her head was thick and the fugue fog heavy. She noticed the sun was well risen so they had obviously let her sleep in. She had no recall of reading for half the night or of her moonlit meanderings. The chocolate was gone and the book lay abandoned on the bedside table where it had been put by the night nurse.

She wandered lost along the corridor looking for something. The day nurse steered her by the elbow into the dining room. She sat befuddled and started a conversation to a fascinating old gentleman, Edward, who told her the same old oral tradition treasures he had unearthed for her before on numerous occasions. He would have been a handsome chap but age had stolen his burly stature and left him withered up. He had a slightly sloping forehead, very little hair as a curtain around his bald patch, lots of age spots on his wizened head and hands as if he had spent most of his life outside. But he still had bright eyes twinkling from the leathery wrinkled depths. They chatted away and Mrs. Morton thoroughly enjoyed herself. He invited her into the sitting room to watch the daily soaps. Someone tried to explain the gist of the story to her but she just nodded her head until she'd nodded off to sleep.

In the corridor, Jennifer was asking after her Mother.

"She stayed up half the night, reading and wandering around, one of the nurses has made a note that she should be banned from reading anything but magazines. Anyway, you'll find her in the day room." The kindly matron filled her in.

"You know my wishes on that, let her have some pleasure, she's worked hard for it." She turned and went in search of her Mother.

"Mother," Jennifer whispered, "just popped in on my way past, how are you?" she touched her arm.

"Oh, hello, dear," she started awake, "Do I know you? Is it luncheon time?"

"Of course you know me; I'm your daughter, Jennifer. It's ok, Mum. It's past lunch time. You'll be fine." She reassured her but felt she really needed it herself. It troubled her so much to see her Mother like this, in such a mental muddle. A moment later a flicker of recognition fleetingly crossed her face.

"I'm ok, but . . ." she leant in conspiratorially, "you've got to get me out of here, I don't belong here, something's missing." These days were the hardest ones on Jennifer, when her own Mother didn't even recognise her. She felt guilty, knowing that if she was at home she probably wouldn't wander around feeling lost, as much, looking for the missing puzzle pieces of her life. But it was also on these days that she knew she'd done the right thing by placing her in this home because she simply couldn't give her the competent, 24 hour/7 days a week care that she required.

"Come on, Mother, let's get you back to your bed for a rest." Jennifer offered her arm as support.

"I'm not tired, dear; I think I'll just sit in my chair by the window." Mrs. Morton told her, pragmatically.

"I best be off," Jennifer glanced at her watch conscious that she had intended it to be a quick visit.

"As you wish, dear." Mrs. Morton replied with indifference, then unexpectedly and quite out of character blew sweet innocent childlike kisses off her gnarled fingertips.

She sat there immobilised by inertia. She found herself mentally wandering corridors searching faces, endlessly wandering, endlessly searching. She felt like she was being pulled down into a dark vortex of depression. She mustn't get sucked down that hole, she vaguely remembered a time in her life when she was so low she was almost buried.

Thankfully, to her delight the sweet, merry twittering of the birds roused her from her reverie. She gave thanks for the window and her cherished vista onto the courtyard. The birds were bopping about in the flowers and occasionally perched precariously on the side of the fountain for a drink or a quick dip. Mesmerized she felt she could enjoy the birds forever.

She remembered that in spring last year, she had conspired with one of her grandchildren . . . yes, it was a grandchild, she felt an electric impulse confirming such a commodity as a grandchild . . . to smuggle in some meadow mix flower seeds-the connection was hazy . . . she couldn't remember which one, she seemed to have lots of grandchildren who she rarely saw-but she . . . yes, it was a girl . . . she felt sure . . . had been sweet enough to put aside her teenage body fixations for long enough to humour her. The gardener had observed their covert operation and deliberately not disturbed the space directly outside her window. As a result she'd had a continuous mass of changing colour of cornflowers, love-in-the-mist, poppies, heartsease, hollyhocks and dianthus. They brought her so much joy and the company of the birds; she really felt she would have gone mad had it not been for this window onto the courtyard.

She cradled a heavy book in her lap, one which had been resting on her bedside table and she sat doodling in the frontispage. She felt inspired to write a poem. Words fleeted through her mind, her mind meandered. The phrase, 'He'd probably set his cap for you if he wasn't already . . .' What was the word? She pondered the vague vast wasteland that was now her disassociated mind, as Lethe-logica crept in. She stared aimlessly at the shaft of light shining in and the doodles turned to words . . . *The particles dance in the light and I get acquainted with the dust fairy. My pen plays pointlessly on the page and I befriend the paper elf* . . . suddenly a bright moment descended and she wrote,

To My Dear Granddaughter, Caitlyn, Thank you for helping me make a secret garden, you have no idea how much it means to me. I want you to have this book with my love, Nanna XOX

As she wrote this shaky dedication she felt alive and lucid but as soon as she'd finished she stared out the window engulfed by bewilderment.

CHAPTER
SIX

Bejewelled Dream

Woken at dawn by the incessant, coarse cry of a juvenile wattle bird, drinking the nectar from a Camilla bush in the courtyard, Mrs. Morton lay in the cosy warmth of her bed enjoying the sweetness of waking up with the creatures of her world. She reached for her glass of water, knocking her book to the ground and this in turn jogged her memory that she had been reading. She scanned the pages to see if she could recall where she was. But, alas, she couldn't. Although one sentence leapt out at her, and lead her on.

There was a knock at the door; Beatty answered it to find Robin.

"Good evening, Beatty, how do you do?" He asked in a quiet voice, squeezing his cap in his hands.

"Who is it, and what do they want?" Mother called from the kitchen.

"It's Robin," she called back, then asked "Will you come in?"

"Yes, briefly."

Good evening greetings were exchanged.

"Mrs . . . Joyce, my Mother has invited Beatty to tea, she said that this evening suits her, would that be okay?"

"Well, I suppose so; you must walk her home and be back by half past nine, she has school tomorrow."

They walked in the cool October air, Robin casually draped his arm around Beatty's shoulders, making her breathing quicken.

"You'll be getting sick of all this walking around after me, I reckon, won't you, Robin?" Beatty asked from the musky crook of his arm.

He stopped walking; placed his hands on her shoulders and said, "I would walk to the ends of the earth to be with you, my darling. I think I'm falling for you, Beatty. I really think you're the bee's knees, you know I truly like your company."

"Robin, you're making me blush, I think I could be falling for you, too. I know I've never felt this way about anyone ever before." Beatty felt shy and looked down. They proceeded, holding hands.

A few blocks away, around the corner from the honey factory was his little home, a terrace house similar to her own, but with only Robin and his Mum in it, it seemed quite clean and spacious. Beatty's eyes boggled at the glass fronted cabinets on the walls filled with assorted collections. Mavis Brownell had a large collection of ceramic shoes and it was Bob's passion to collect owl ornaments for which he felt an affinity. She tried not to be rude, but felt compelled to look at the amassed objects.

Robin pushed her along gently in the small of her back, manoeuvering her into the sitting room where his mother sat, rapidly knitting, a record played on the gramophone.

"Mum, this is Beatty," Robin said putting a protective arm around her, "Beatty, this is me Mum, Mavis Brownell."

"Good Evening, Mrs. Brownell, pleased to meet you, how do you do?" said Beatty.

"I'm quite well lass, but for heaven's sakes call me Mavis, I've heard so much about you, the boss's daughter n all, Robin can't stop talking about you, n I feel I already know you. Take a seat both of you."

They sat in unison. There were so many plump tapestry cushions on the overstuffed ottoman that there was hardly room left for people so they perched on the edge. She placed her feet on a colourful, oval rag-rug, clearly Mavis was very crafty. While Mavis knitted she continued to chat away putting them both at ease. The record came to an end scratching a monotonous loop and requiring attention.

"Sorry, Robin, can you get that? I'm forgetting my manners, I just made a simple tea of egg sandwiches and currant brownies, hope that's ok?" Mavis left the room to make a pot of tea and bring the plate in. "Since Bob went off to war, it's been pretty informal around here, Robin n I usually have a simple meal on our laps. I hope that suits you, too."

"It's nice and homely, sort of friendly-like," agreed Beatty. They chatted amicably, with Mavis doing most of the babbling.

Robin watched the grandfather clock in the corner and just before nine he cleared his throat and said they needed to be off.

"I think she likes you, what did you think of her?" Robin asked as they walked slowly along.

"She's nice but she sure talks a lot." Beatty replied.

"Oh, she only does that when she's a bit wound up; she misses Dad n gets a bit lonely for company, that's all."

He pulled her under the cover of a shop awning, and kissed her.

"Sometimes at night I think I'll burst with the love I feel for you, honey." He unbuttoned her coat and slipped his arms into the inviting warmth where he excitedly stroked her through her dress.

"Stop it, Robin, we shouldn't, you know it's a sin!" she tried to push him away.

"Doesn't feel like a sin to me, sweetie."

"No, it doesn't really to me either. But I've got to get home, what will Mother say?" Beatty dreamily gave in and kissed back, hidden in the shadows of the night.

"Come on then, I best get you back." They heard the distant town clock strike half past nine. "Or your Mother won't let me take you out again."

Feeling dishevelled Beatty smoothed down her hair then tucked her arm in his and they walked briskly back.

Beatty's Mother was irritable when she arrived home; having had to get the unruly children off to bed when usually of late that had been Beatty's undertaking.

"You're late," she announced.

"Only by five minutes."

"Still, don't let it happen again."

No matter how much she helped out it never seemed to be good enough for her Mother, she quickly brushed her teeth and snuggled into bed wanting to savour the sweetness of Robin's words and kisses.

Beatty made an effort to get home from work in good time the next day to play with her siblings. On the front path she played marbles with Harry, and the twins, winning his favourite biggest cobalt blue one, his prize tom bowler, but she gave it back when they had finished. She played elastics with Amelia, and momentarily they shared a rare sense of companionship and she was just getting puffed and thinking of knocking off because it was getting too dark when Mother called them in for tea-time.

After tea she gave Evie a bath in the wooden laundry trough. She soaped up her perfect little body, revelling in the pleasure that Evie derived by squeezing water over her shoulders. Wrapped in a towel, Beatty dried her by the open door of the combustion oven. Mother organised her napkin and nightie. Freshly powdered and pink cheeked she was passed around everyone for a good night cuddle and kiss, then back to Beatty who fed her the evening bottle and sang her to sleep. Beatty lay her warm, cuddly body down in her cradle and felt a rush of adoration for her. Back in the kitchen Mother said to Gran, "Good, that's one down, five to go." Beatty was hurt to be calculated with the younger children. However, she still offered to read a chapter of 'A Secret Garden' and the boys jumped up and down with enthusiasm. They all gathered on her bed and when she read that Mary found the key to the secret garden the boys cheered her on.

"Hush, boys, or Mum will make you go to bed, without the rest of the chapter." She whispered in a conspiratorial tone.

The children relaxed and lazed on her bed as they listened to the unfolding of the story. Gregory picked his nose absentmindedly and they all scratched their heads, from time to time. Amelia laid her head in Beatty's lap basking in the new found friendship they had shared earlier. She shuddered and started to vigorously scratch her scalp, until she had drawn blood. Beatty paused in her reading and looked under Amelia's fingernails at the blood and noticed something odd.

Suddenly, Beatty jumped up, "Mum, 'Melia's got nits," she called out frantically.

Mother dropped her knitting and came in to inspect Amelia's thick auburn hair. On close scrutiny the coppery colour was streaked with thick white nits, encrusted close to her scalp. The biggest lice she had ever seen were burrowing in for a drink of blood. Mother nearly fainted. Gran bustled in and was horrified.

"How in the world did we miss this til now Joyce?" she asked.

"I simply don't know, I guess I haven't been a very good mother lately, since Charles went away I've been beside myself with worry."

It was in a rare moment of honesty that Joyce recognised her despondency.

"Beatty, you'll have to have the day off school tomorrow, Harry can take a note explaining all your absences, so as you can help get the head lice out of the children's hair and we'll have to boil the bedding to make sure it's not got any hiding away inside it to re-infest us all." Gran said taking charge of the situation. Beatty scratched her head, not sure if she could really feel anything or if was sympathetic itching, "Could you take a look at me, too, Gran?" she asked.

"Yes, dear," she said parting Beatty's long wavy locks, "Sure enough, though I dare say we all do to a greater or lesser degree." She withdrew a louse and squashed it between her fingernails.

Mrs. Morton felt incredibly itchy. She reached over for the nurse's buzzer and gave it a lingering push. She'd scratched her scalp through her thin grey hair and drew blood, then scratched raised red welts on her face and arms. A breathless nurse arrived, flustered by what she saw but relieved on closer inspection to see she was alright, if somewhat flushed.

"What's the matter, what can I do for you, Mrs. Morton?" she inquired.

"The bed needs changing and I want a shower, I have lice, they're crawling all over me."

"Settle down, dear, I'm sure you don't but I'll help organise your shower."

She helped her sit on the shower stool and handed her the hand-held shower nozzle, with tepid water flowing.

"Will you be right dear while I make your bed fresh?" she asked.

"Yes, thankyou." Mrs. Morton turned the hot up as soon as the nurse turned her back, 'I'll kill those blighters,' she muttered.

Settled back in her bed, she felt much more comfortable and continued reading.

The next morning Mother was even more efficient, than her old self. She bustled about the kitchen boiling water in every available receptacle. She instructed everyone to strip their beds and take their sheets out for a good shaking. Gran was already bent over the copper, the diluted caustic soda stinging her eyes, plunging the bedding with an old dolly. Mother delegated the job of wringing to Beatty. Washing the bedding was such a big job in their primitive lean-to wash-house, that had Father ever participated she was sure they would have had a more modern set-up by now. Usually, they only washed the bedding once a fortnight, alternating so that there were only four sets a week to do. Thankfully, Beatty looked about; there wasn't a cloud in the sky, so it would be a good drying day. Mother wrote a note for Harry to deliver to the school, and Beatty wrote one to Mrs. Richardson and quietly slipped it to him to deliver on his way there, bribing him to keep quiet with the promise of a bag of boiled sweets.

When Beatty had a break at morning tea, Mother was making a list of tasks at hand.

She went to the house-keeping tin, and found it was again inexplicably heavier; a puzzled frown crossed her face. "Ma, do you know anything about how this extra money appears in the tin? You haven't hocked anything at the pawn shop, have you?"

"Of course not, Joyce, you know I rarely go out!" Gran Flo exploded.

"What about you, Beatty?" Mother asked.

"Well, I . . ."

"Out with it girl, did Robin pay you extra?"

"Yes, that's it," Beatty grabbed the lifeline, not wanting to outright lie but also not wanting to jeopardise her job, "I gave you most of it,

51

but kept a few pennies back as pocket money, then I felt guilty and put them in too. Don't be mad, I was just trying to help out, I know the pension is pittance."

"Ok, I know you're a good girl really. Now, listen carefully, I want you to take the tram into town, take my pocket book to the bank, get out some of the pension and get some important supplies. We need some methylated spirits, a fine tooth comb, more caustic soda and a few other things that I've written here, also, take the Box Brownie camera in so they can get the film out and process it and put a replacement one in."

She handed her the purse, bank pocketbook, the heavy camera, a list and tram timetable as well as two string bags for supplies.

"When you get home we'll treat everybody's heads."

Beatty walked the streets, enjoying the sun on her back, tempted to go via the honey factory but deciding against it as it was a bit out of the way. She waited at the tram stop, as she didn't have a watch she asked a kindly old gentleman the time. He told her it was twenty-to-eleven. She was a bit nervous but also excited as this was her first trip into town all by herself.

She liked travelling by tram but it was a rare treat. Only on the odd occasion did they ever have to venture past their fairly self contained suburb, there was the corner store, the butchers, school and the library all within walking distance.

The tram rumbled along and Beatty gazed around, drinking in the new buildings since she last came this way. She had also brought with her the little nest egg she'd saved up. Untying the white lace edged handkerchief she re-counted her savings. She hoped she had enough to buy the Christmas presents she'd planned. She knew she was early but this was a perfect opportunity, and so unexpected.

She quickly made the purchases on the list from her Mother, dropped the film in for processing, paying for it and asking to have the photos posted out when ready. Then she went into a haberdashery shop, where the smell of new fabrics greeted her, the calicos and linens smelt especially welcoming. At the counter she asked for a foot of fine white lawn, she also chose out three embroidery silks, mauve, pink and green for the ladies and a red one the colour of a robin's breast for Robin. She would make hand rolled edges on handkerchiefs with their initials embroidered in the corners.

Next she walked into a large department store looking for the toy section. She was overwhelmed by the colours and choices of dolls, soldiers, trains and teddy bears. She wanted to buy one of each. There was a display of seed packets on the counter so she chose one for each sibling, practical vegetable seed for the boys and flowers for the girls. Knowing she had limited time, she enquired about marbles for the boys. A drawer with many partitions was pulled out and Beatty looked in astonishment at the huge assortment of colourful marbles. She bought a bag of small ones which she would divide between her three younger brothers and also one highly desirable tom bowler each. As Beatty was about to leave, she noticed something in the glass fronted display cabinet, it was a koala 'bear' made from real kangaroo fur and with it's head slightly on the side it looked like it was appealing to her to take him home. He was simply adorable. She asked the price then counted out the last of her money and realised she could just manage it, this one present cost almost more than all the others put together, but she knew she just *had* to buy it for Evie.

She dashed out and arrived just in time to catch the tram. On the way home she thought how much fun it had been to buy presents with money she had earned herself, they were simple but they would be a surprise, she still had to make some of them with the materials she'd bought, but Christmas was still six weeks away.

There was a tentative knock on the door, "Mother, are you awake?" Concerned by her Mother's confusion of yesterday, Jennifer was dutifully checking on her condition whilst dashing between shopping chores.

"Yes, dear, come in." She ha-hummed to clear her throat and took a sip of water.

"I brought you a sprig of Daphne, because I know you like it so much, did you sleep well?"

"Much better, thank you, dear." She closed her eyes and breathed in a deep draught of the heavenly lemony fragrance.

Jennifer rummaged around in her massive bag and brought out a Dream Book. "Oh and here's your dream interpretations book, I borrowed it."

"That's funny, dear; I thought you had already returned it." Mrs Morton shook her head in bewilderment; sometimes with lucid windows of clarity she could swear that people deliberately played games with her recall just to befuddle her. In her frustration she blurted out, "For heaven's sake stop treating me like a child!"

Later in the day, Laura came in to check on her and tidy up, she chatted amicably and finding both the dream book still out and Mrs Morton in a relatively lucid state, asked, "You're something of a dream interpretation expert, aren't you?"

"At times I have been, dear."

"I've been having a recurring dream; perhaps I could look it up?"

"Why don't you tell it to me dear?"

Laura quietly closed the door and settled herself on the edge of the bed, smoothing down the bedspread before she sat down. "I dream that I am walking to my abode which is a cave in the mountains, I know it is home because I really have a sense that I want to get there. But, I can't get there, the path has collapsed in many places and great big gaps of earth are exposed. I turn to go back the way that I came but in the way, on the path I have just walked is a death adder about to strike. I quickly raise my hands in prayer position and say, 'Namaste', and to my relief it goes away. Beads and gemstones start to drizzle down from the sky. I go down to the stream and get a basin of water and wash in it, discarding the used water over a cliff, I almost slip but then I usually wake feeling a bit startled. What do you think?"

"Well, dear, it seems to me that someone you trust will betray you, my advice is, watch your back, it'll work out well in the end, because it sort of has a positive ending. Don't fret, dear."

"Wow, you are good at interpreting, thanks, I feel better, now." Laura stood and ran her hand over the cover of the dream book before slotting it into its spot on the book shelf.

CHAPTER
SEVEN

Alcheringa

Mrs Morton settled down with her book, 'where was I?' she wondered, that's right, the family has to be deloused.

Everyone was gathered around the kitchen table eating honey on bread and waiting for Beatty when she arrived.

"Mmm," Mrs Morton mumbled, "I wouldn't mind a piece of fresh bread and honey myself. Perhaps I should ask that nice nurse to bring me some." She resumed reading and that thought just slipped away into the oblivious avalanche of Alzheimer's.

Beatty quietly slipped her purchases under her pillow as she walked past the grey blanket wall.

"What took you so long, girl?" Mother snapped in her weariness.

"I didn't know where everything was so I wasted a bit of time looking, I suppose."

In the backyard, the sheets flapping and cracking merrily in the wind, they set up a production line to treat all the heads. With three kitchen chairs in a row, firstly, Mother cut the hair with her heavy dress making scissors, next Gran applied methylated spirits to fry and drown the lice and Beatty was in third position with the fine tooth comb and the arduous task of combing out the nits.

As Beatty was tugging through Amelia's thick bob of hair, she broke out in a cold sweat as she recalled a reoccurring nightmare she had in which she wakes to find her Mother lopping off her long hair, her shining crowning glory. She was sure that her Mother was jealous of her luxurious mass of waves because as she'd had more children her own beautiful tresses had thinned and gone limp.

All the younger children were done and it was Beatty's turn. As her Mother approached with the heavy dress making scissors, Beatty pleaded with her not to take off too much. Joyce absentmindedly cut Beatty's hair so that the edges were lopsided.

"Here, give me those," Gran elbowed her way in, snatching the scissors from her daughter. In trying to even up the sides she made Beatty's hair into a bob cut. Beatty was on the verge of tears. The acrid smell and sting of the methylated spirits was an assault on Beatty's scalp.

"Robin's here!" called Amelia, "He's coming through."

Beatty's tears burst their flood gates and poured forth down her cheeks. She was mortifyingly embarrassed for Robin to see her in this state, if only the ground would open up and shallow her whole!

"Go away, Robin, now isn't a good time, can't you tell?" said Gran.

"So . . . sorry, b-but it looks good, Bea, don't fret, I'll duck out the front to give the boys that game of marbles I promised."

Both women worked on her hair and after combing it through they even shampooed the metho smell out, something they hadn't done for the younger ones. The theory being that if only rinsed, leaving some smell behind there was less chance of being re-infected. Beatty helped check both her Mother and Gran, who neither had many nor with their hair cut shoulder length and not being as thick wasn't as difficult. "There's a lot to be said for keeping the hair tied back in a bun." They agreed. Beatty mused that hers was now too short for a chignon.

Robin came back through to the back yard and said, "I wonder if I could take Beatty, that's if she wants to, and Harry, of course for a drive and a picnic by the river at the foothills of the Dandenong Ranges, I'll get them home before dark."

"Yes, I don't see why not, mind you don't wear out the Ford with too many unnecessary trips though, lad, we can't afford for anything to go wrong with it."

In the cab of the truck, Beatty sat in the middle, squeezed between the boys, with a basket of fresh baked goodies on her lap. Robin hastily planted a kiss on her cheek.

They rumbled along enjoying the sun streaming in. Beatty's usually wavy hair with all the length and weight chopped off it was starting to spring into curls. It felt so light and free, she couldn't help running her fingers through it.

In a shady glade they spread out the blanket and sat down, when Harry'd had his fill of currant buns he wandered off nearby. Beatty and Robin sat swatting mozzies that buzzed around them incessantly, and sneaking the odd kiss while keeping half an eye on Harry.

Suddenly, Harry screamed and slipped on the rocks into the river, Robin ran down and helped to pull him out. Sodden but safe on the riverbank, they wrung out the boys' clothes and draped them in the nearby trees to flap dry, they stretched out to warm on the blanket.

"Not a word to your Mother, lad, do you hear?" Robin warned.

"No fear, I won't tell." Harry stammered through chattering teeth.

The afternoon shadows were lengthening and they packed up for a quiet uneventful trip home.

As Robin was dropping them home he said, "A word, Beatty, before you go . . ." Harry slammed the door. "You sure look cute with your hair like that," he cupped the back of her head and kissed her, "I just want you to know, I think I'm falling in love with you."

"Mmm, I think I might be falling in love with you, too." A loud clunk startled them, Robin leapt out of the truck to see Gregory and Rupert slinking away, a prize tom bowler, abandoned in the gutter and a ding in the paint work interrupted the mellow mood.

"I best be off, I promised Mum I'd give her a hand to stack firewood out the back. Hope to see you on the week-end. Perhaps we could go to the flicks?"

"That would be lovely, thanks for today." Beatty swished her curls and bounded inside, filled with renewed vigour and resolve to help with the evening routine.

The kitchen was a buzzing hive of activity, with dinner being served and the clanking and clattering of activity. They chatted amicably about the excursion and Beatty offered to bathe Evie and read to the children in her fresh bed. She really enjoyed giving Evie her bath in the laundry trough, Evie was so cooperative and Beatty revelled in her soft, adorable body. She wrapped her in a towel and dried her in the kitchen. As she lay her down to put her night napkin on she noticed that she had a bad napkin rash and that her tummy wasn't soft as usual but rough and sandpapery, "Mum, can you pass me the honey and calendula cream for Evie's bottom?" and she applied a liberal amount. Evie, usually so good natured was fractious.

"You're tired aren't you bubs?" She said as she picked her up and Evie lay her head on her shoulder.

When all the chores were done, the girls rosy cheeked in their sweet smelling nighties and the boys looking clean, neat and combed in their fresh pyjamas, they all snuggled on Beatty's bed.

The women in the next room were enormously relieved to put their feet up after their busy day.

"Now, where were we?" asked Beatty.

A cacophony of differing answers filled her ears, she herself had been so busy and distracted lately she could barely remember, "Oh, that's right, she hears wailing in the corridors at night and the nurse insists it is the wind but she thinks it sounds like a child's cry, let's see if she's right."

She read, animated, and drew the children into the world of Mary Lennox, the robin red breast and the secret garden. As the children grew tired their heads began to nod and their eyes glazed over and became hooded.

Everyone was startled awake by a knock at the door. Beatty twisted and pulled back the heavy blackout curtain, to her disquiet she saw Mrs Richardson, standing with her arms crossed. Immediately Beatty had a queasy feeling as if someone had punched her in the stomach. She heard her Mother answer the door, saw Mrs Richardson nod and enter, she heard her lead her through to the sitting room.

Mother called, "Beatrice, you best come here."

Abruptly Beatty pulled herself away and whispered in hushed urgency, "Go to bed now, not a peep, I'll read more tomorrow."

Beatty entered the sitting room as anxiously as a timid virgin on her wedding night. The air could be cut with a knife.

Mother said, "Mrs Richardson says there's been an outbreak of Scarlet Fever, her little ones are sick and she wants you to run the library, in her absence, but I'm not sure you could manage it."

Beatty gasped for breath, relieved that it wasn't a personal attack but also concerned for Mrs Richardson, who she had grown to respect, as well as for Mrs Richardson's children and also for her siblings who played with Mrs Richardson's after church every Sunday.

Beatty was so thankful that Mrs Richardson hadn't given away her secret employment. She looked at her Mother, "I could do it, I know I could, please let me help out."

"What about your schooling, you're so close to your teaching exam? I'm not sure, you've been so busy already." Mother shifted her weight from one foot to the other, undecided.

"I could study in the library when we aren't busy, I know I can manage, also the money would be useful, wouldn't it?" She answered her Mother, then turning to Mrs Richardson she asked, "So, how *are* your children?"

"Well, my youngest is the sickest, but the doctor says she'll be fine. That's right I meant to ask you, do you know where the Aboriginal Medicine Woman lives since she moved from her spot up the Yarra, she is supposed to be living in a humpy nearby here? I've heard she has some herbal bush medicine to break a fever."

"No, we won't have anything to do with Abo quacks, but you could ask Mrs Parker next door she makes it her business to know everybody else's business."

"Ok, will do, well I best hurry, got to get home to my children. I'll see you at the library at eight am sharp, tomorrow, Beatrice to show you what to do."

"Yes, good night, Mrs Richardson," Beatty let her out, then gave a 'whoop' of joy.

"You mustn't celebrate the misfortune of others Beatrice May!" Mother scolded. Instantly, the wind collapsed from Beatty's sails. She went to bed chastised but excited as well and she lay awake for hours.

Beatty woke with a start remembering she had to get up and go to the library, to be in charge and run it for the first time. She dressed in her Sunday best, with the white lace collar at her throat. Pity her hair was too short to go up in a chignon she thought, because then I'd really look like a proper librarian.

Beatty arrived before Mrs Richardson, and let herself in and started chores. When Mrs Richardson arrived she was flustered and explained, "I won't stay long, I've been up all night with my little Alice, she's pulled through and I want to get home to her. You've proved yourself a sensible girl, Beatrice, I trust you to run this place to a high standard and continue to keep it clean. I'll call in again in a few days to see how you are doing."

Any fantasies of studying were soon dashed as Beatty found herself engrossed in her work of sorting books, filing cards, helping patrons and dusting and cleaning. Just when she thought she would be able to settle to study someone interrupted her with an enquiry.

The older people she knew from church asked after her family and wanted to chat. Mid afternoon when Beatty was seated at the counter concentrating on paperwork, she smelt an odd, overwhelming smell and looked up, to her surprise there was a wild looking Aboriginal woman who had stealthily crept in standing in front of the counter.

She gave Beatty a grin, showing lots of missing teeth and the teeth that remained were stained with pituri, a chewing tobacco mix. She wore no respectable clothing to speak of, an old shift dress which she tugged down to barely cover her rear elevation leaving lots of dusty ochre red skin showing. Her pendulous breasts and protruding abdomen clearly showed through the fine worn out fabric.

"Good afternoon," Beatty said, shutting her gaping mouth and remembering her manners. She's never been this close to an Aborigine, let alone held a conversation.

"Bag take 'um." The generous lips mouthed.

"What is it?" Beatty asked.

"Is dem bush herbs and dried apple bush, to bring down bad high fever spirit down, Ms old library lady asks for, you give her?"

"Sure, I will, what does she do with them and who shall I say brought them?"

By now all the other patrons had vacated the library due to the stench of the bush woman.

"Tell her boil up and give tea with lots of honey to take em bad taste away. It will help with fever and sore throat, help child breathe easier. I 'Kabbarli' mean 'Grandmother' to my people but most white people call me 'Lena'. I medicine woman. Me father trained me when all his sons die. There had to be someone to carry on the traditions even if it make em spirits restless to have a girl learn, they understand now."

Beatty was intrigued despite all her Mother's warnings not to associate with the 'Abos'. This was a highly intelligent woman, if somewhat lacking in social graces.

"So, where do you live?"

"My people are 'Wirongi tribe' who live near Yuria Waters, long walkabout away, but I moved to collect herbs and bush tucker, lived in a humpy up the Yarra for while now down by river not far from here. De Yarra no good now, 'yarra' word mean 'flowing water' to my people but now it slowing and muddy. White people pollute everywhere they go, spoil Alcheringa, I move on."

"What exactly is in the bag?" Beatty asked.

"Is good, dried leaves and roots to scare off spirit of fever, work real good, boil up and drink, work good, not to worry, is not poison."

"What's this 'Alcheringa' you talk about?"

"Is de dreamtime, Alcheri means dream, if people not live in harmony, day turn dream to nightmare."

Without saying 'Goodbye' Kabbarli Lena, turned and was gone as quietly as she had arrived. Beatty got out the broom and swept the trail of debris up, wiped up the dusty footprints and grabbed a cloth to polish the counter to a high sheen, putting the leaking bag into a sturdy plastic bag. She felt a strong urge to disinfect everything but despite that found she had enjoyed her chat to the medicine woman and found her a fascinating person. She was bursting with questions to ask, but she doubted she would ever see her again.

Robin was outside waiting to pick her up so she requested they go via Mrs Richardson's house to drop off the package with instructions.

Laura was doing her last round before knocking off and got a surprise to see Mrs Morton still awake and reading, she looked up when she sensed movement.

"I thought you would have read yourself to sleep by now, Mrs Morton."

"No, I'm engrossed in my book. I wonder, dear, if you have any Aboriginal blood in you? What with your lovely olive tan, your dark wild hair and your broad nose."

"Yes, we do, it's a distant link and hard to trace through the stolen generation but my grandmother was quite strongly Aboriginal looking." She straightened up the bed, she loved chatting to Mrs Morton in her more lucid moments but now at the end of her shift she was tired and just wanted to go home to sleep. "Can I get you a sleeping tablet?"

"No, I'm fine, I'll read for a while longer."

CHAPTER
EIGHT

Spring Meadow

A week later, Beatty was busy going about her routine at the library when Harry burst in, "Beatty, guess what?"

"What, Harry, it better be important, I'm working."

"Yeah, it is, Beatty, school's been shut down due to an outbreak of Scarlet Fever, fair dinkum, I'm not telling fibbers."

"Well, I never," Beatty clasped hold of the counter, her mind doing overtime, "You wouldn't read about it."

Harry started tugging on her sleeve, "Shove off now, kiddo, I've got work to do." She exclaimed in her exasperation.

Not long after, the Health Inspector arrived with the official notification. He said in his neatly clipped accent, "The library will be closing due to health concerns until further notice, please kindly see your patrons out and affix this notice to the door. Good morning to you."

Beatty was glad to have had prior warning as she felt quite faint. She dutifully finished off and locked up. The streets were deserted, all the shops shut and the people had obviously cloistered themselves away in fear of the dreaded lurgy. Beatty strolled home, disappointed by the turn of events and concerned by the possible implications.

Robin hastened around after work when he heard the news on the bush telegraph; an old codger had called into the honey factory on his way past and delivered the info.

The adults sat around the kitchen table solemnly conversing while the younger kids tore around playing tag enjoying a holiday mood.

Robin suggested that he, Beatty, Harry and Amelia should go up to check on the bees and add extra boxes.

"I don't wanna go; it would be too squishy in the truck for all of us, anyway," called Amelia from the next room.

"True it would, but otherwise it seems like a good opportunity, while school is shut and no work for Beatty at the library," said Gran.

"Ok, I'll pack a tin of bully beef and some of Mum's currant slice for lunch and be around at sparrow's . . . chirp, first thing in the morning. He very nearly said, 'sparrow's fart' but luckily checked himself in time.

Beatty felt despondent when she went to bed but by morning she was filled with excitement and enthusiasm to be going on another adventure, even if it was a working one, with Robin.

They swung by the factory in the morning to load up the super boxes and set off towards the honey meadows. Robin drove skirting the main city of Melbourne, through Sunshine and Melton South. At Baccus Marsh he pulled over and said, "Swap places with you Beatty, I'll teach you to drive."

"No, Robin, I could never drive." Beatty didn't know many women at all who drove and assumed it was men's business.

"C'mon, Beat, it'll be good for you." Robin urged.

They swapped spots and Robin explained the basics. Beatty was terribly nervous as she kangaroo hopped at the side of the road.

"Bloomin' heck, Beatty, I could do better than that," exclaimed Harry, "Let me out!"

Once she was moving it wasn't too bad, still terribly nerve wracking and jolting so she drove as slow as a wet week but she quite enjoyed the rush of excitement she felt. She turned onto a rough dirt road at a sign pointing to Blackwood and Lerderderg National Park and jerked over the potholes until they came to Greendale and the new location of the bee hives.

They got out of the truck, had a stretch and started to gown up in their whites and veils to get to work. As they approached the bee hives, a strong sense of apprehension descended on them. From a distance everything looked intact but as they approached there was something definitely wrong. The silence was deafening. The reassuring hum of the usual buzz of activity, bees cheerfully collecting nectar, was absent. A queer chill ran a shiver up their spines. It was as if they were walking through a deserted ghost town. Something was definitely wrong. The hives appeared abandoned. Eerie! Robin lifted the lid of the closest box with his curved hive tool. A fine powdery mould filled Beatty's nostrils, making her want to sneeze. The propolis seal cracked as he lifted out one of the frames.

There, the embryonic larvae lay curled up, suspended in the comb, putrefying yet preserved like the bodies in the ashes at Pompeii. This eerie other worldly sensations made Beatty feel sick to her stomach. Robin and Beatty looked at each other, fear and dread filling their eyes. Brood disease? Every beekeeper's nightmare!

"Well, I'll be damned, I'm blowed if I haven't let down your Dad and the whole blessed lot of you, we're ruined Beatty, done for." Robin shook his head in disbelief.

Mrs. Morton felt restless, slipped out of bed, feeling the cool lino under her feet. She stealthily crept out of her room and wandered along the deserted corridor. An attendant linked arms with her and steered her back to bed. As she settled back in bed and resumed reading she didn't feel anywhere near as befuddled as she did wandering the passageway.

Robin collapsed on the ground with his head in his hands in despair, "Oh, B-bea, I've really b-blown it. Your D-dad had the b-business for so many years, b-building it up from scratch. He loved those b-bees. Then I'm left in charge for just a few months and I ruin it all." His nervous stutter returned haunting him in his anxiety.

Beatty knelt down beside him, wrapped her arms around him and cradled his head against her bosom, "Come now, Robin, Brood disease is just that," she comforted, "a disease, it can strike anytime, it's not your fault."

"That's b-bulldust, B-beatty, obviously I'm the one that placed the bee boxes in the shade, not following your Dad's directions, it was too cold and damp for the bees, it compromised their health and let down their immunity-don't you see, there's nothing that can be done, I've completely ruined it."

Harry was playing a curious game of a cross between cricket and tennis nearby with a branch and some gum nuts.

"Come on Robin, let's go for a little walk and decide what we have to do next."

They wandered across the paddocks, through the waist high grass until they came to an old cottage used for hay storage. It was quaint but a long time since it had been inhabited. There was an overgrown Daphne plant by the door and the remnants of choked spring bulbs, once someone's pride and joy. The citrus-y sweet fragrance filled the air.

Beatty broke off a sprig and handed it to Robin reassuring him that everything would be alright.

They looked around in the cottage and Robin pulled Beatty down onto a bale, kissing her.

"Robin, don't, there's probably mice."

"Don't worry Beatty, they won't tell. I really need you now Beatty."

She surrendered to his passionate persuasion. He tried to be gentle but it still hurt and before she knew it, it was over. Robin lay spent on top of her. He moved to the side and cradled her, apologising softly.

They dozed off to sleep in each other arms.

She is walking in a spring meadow with wild flowers all around, she is barefoot and the grass is heavy with dew. She drops her purse, as the coins roll out they turn into hopping rabbits. To her surprise the rabbits mate copiously and rapidly.

Beatty woke with a gasp, breathless and ashamed to witness the sex act in her dream even if it was only rabbits. She lay in the crook of Robin's arm with heightened mindfulness. Listening for Harry and mice, keenly aware of the aching in her womb, the tremendous burden of guilt. She silently prayed, "Blessed Mary, Honoured Mother, forgive my dreams, forgive my dreams, forgive my dreams . . . . forgive my sins . . ." The litany ran around her head like a record stuck in a groove.

"Robin, what have we done?" she said rousing him.

He startled awake to see how upset Beatty was, "Don't cry, Bea it'll be ok, you'll see. We'll get married and go to Tasmania the Apple Isle for our honey moon, anyway, don't fret, you can't get pregnant the first time you do it. You are ok, aren't you? Are you hurt?" He stroked her face tenderly.

Beatty sniffled then said, "We have to check on Harry."

Harry was nonchalantly fishing in a billabong nearby when they arrived back, totally oblivious to their long absence.

They tied up the boxes and loaded on as many as they could fit, which was about a quarter of the whole colony.

Robin drove back, forgetting his resolve to teach Beatty to drive. A tremendously guilty silence engulfed them.

They unloaded the bee boxes at the factory; they would need checking, cleaning and possibly destroying. Then headed off to tell Beatty's Mother.

With a resolute yet weary mien they walked along the hall, steeling themselves for the inevitable.

"Evening all," Robin said, nodding his head.

"Come in, take a seat, you look done in," Joyce said pulling out a chair.

"No, no, I won't, thanks. I bring bad news, very bad news. I'm so sorry, the bees are gone, and we have the foul brood disease. I'm so sorry. We'll have to make three more trips to collect up all the boxes. Some might be salvageable but we've lost the colony. I should never have put them so close to the trees, should have checked them more thoroughly . . . I don't know what to say, I'm so sorry, I'll try to make it up to you somehow."

The colour drained from Joyce's face and she collapsed onto a chair.

"Get out of my sight, boy. I should have known not to let a boy do a man's job. GO. Shove off. Sod off!"

"You best go now lad, she'll be right. It's such rotten news, it'll take a few days to adjust," Gran explained.

A few days later, Robin tentatively knocked on the door requesting Beatty and Harry's help.

"No, I forbid you to see our Beatty again, Harry can come and give you a hand to finish off, but you stay away from Beatty. You've ruined our family, you understand."

"I-I'm so sorry, Joyce," Robin stammered, hung his head and left.

"Don't you think you're being too hard on the lad? After all, a disease is an act of God," Gran said.

"No, you heard him, he admitted to bad management the other day," Joyce exploded.

Beatty said, "That's not fair, I love Robin," and she threw herself down on her bed, refusing to get up and help with the chores.

Amelia called out, "Beatty won't get up."

"Don't worry, dear, leave her, she's in a mood," Joyce called back.

Both Beatty and Robin, separate and alone with their thoughts wondered how Joyce would have responded had she known the full story of the other day. Shudder and cringe at the thought!

Mrs. Morton had an overwhelming urge to count her money. She got out her purse and decided she needed to make a wish. The coins make a satisfying clink and splash as they hit the water in her porcelain wishing pond, the sanitary abyss of her toilet bowl. She could see water lilies floating on the surface and they bobbed and bowed as she offered them her fortune. She pottered around. Squirreling coins for a rainy day in hidey holes and choc squares for surprise moments. Ohh, she thinks this is so fun, like . . . some festival, that's right, a treasure hunt. Only, by the time she had hidden her treasure she had totally forgotten she was playing. A nurse looked around the door and gently shepherded her back to bed, before organizing her a sleeping tablet.

When she woke next morning she was so groggy, she didn't realise it was late. She sat by the window in her nightie feeling vague and dreamy. She dozed.

In the early evening Laura came by to check on her. By now she felt a bit brighter and asked her, "How are you, dear?"

"I'm well, slept heaps but still a bit tired around the edges," Laura replied.

"I know, I've been in la-la land all day, but I'm better now."

Unbeknownst to them, while they were chatting Kristy had scooped up a handful of 'Sharps', needle syringes from her pocket and planted them in Laura's unzipped handbag. Not long after, as Matron went into the staff kitchen to make a cuppa, she nudged Laura's bag out of the way with her foot, "Messy girl," she mumbled then took a quick intake of breath as sharps tumbled out of her bag. She bent over and scooped them into a bowl, then walked briskly along the corridor to look for Laura.

She popped her head around the corner and said, "Ahh, there you are, Laura, just the person I was looking for. Now, tell me, why have you stolen and hidden sharps in your bag?" she demanded of Laura totally ignoring Mrs Morton's presence.

Laura was puzzled, "I don't know what you're talking about."

"How about I just recovered these from your handbag?"

"I didn't take them," Laura looked directly into Matron's eyes with her lovely wide innocent, fawn-like gaze.

Matron believed her, "Well, if you didn't, who did?"

Laura shook her head, "I don't know."

"Anybody got it in for you?"

"No, I don't think so."

"Well, I'll ask around, I'll find out." Matron turned on her heel and squeaked down the corridor. Laura had little doubt Matron would manage to find the culprit.

"Gosh, Mrs M, it's just like my dream, you know, the one you interpreted, to watch my back."

"So, it is," Mrs Morton agreed obligingly, not too clear about what she was agreeing to.

She cradled her book, reading the same paragraph over and over.

Evie was burning up with Scarlet Fever, she was whimpering in pain. Beatty knew it was all her fault as punishment for her sins. She had to get to confession otherwise Baby Evie would die. She had to get absolution for her sins. It couldn't wait til morning, she had to go now. She grabbed her shawl and stole out of the house.

CHAPTER
NINE

Feverish Dreams

After two consecutive days of helping load up and unload the bee boxes, Harry was exhausted and running a temperature. Robin led him to the door to explain to Joyce. She met him with a curt 'hello'. He straightened his shoulders for courage and cleared his throat.

"Harry, isn't feeling well, I think he needs to rest up. I still have another load to do to finish up, could Beatty come out tomorrow? And Amelia too, of course."

"Haven't you got any mates you could take, instead of my girls?" Joyce snapped.

"Well, no, M'am, all my mates have gone off to do their bit for their country." Robin replied.

"I suppose it has to be done, but you leave our Beatty alone, or I'll tan your hide, you understand?"

"Yes, M'am."

And while she was on a powerful roll she continued, "I forbid Beatrice to have anything to do with you after that."

Next morning, Beatty arose at day break and whispered to Amelia to get up but she mumbled, "Go away, it's not fair; it's far too early, just let me sleep."

"Oh, for heaven's sakes don't make a scene, 'Melia, just get up, c'mon be a good girl," Beatty cajoled.

"No, I won't, I'm tired, let me sleep." She rolled over turning her back on her sister.

Beatty tip-toed through to the kitchen to find her Mother crouched in front of the fire in her nightie, her abdomen swollen with the growing life inside her, blowing and muttering her morning incantation.

"Morning, Mother, Amelia's being a pain, she won't get up."

Mother rose from her squat with great effort, straightened up and waddled along the hall to arouse Amelia. She sat on the side of her bed and stroked her hair and coaxed Amelia, "I'll make you your favourite meal of Yorkshire pudding and gravy, if you get up now, like a good girl."

The girls waited outside with the picnic hamper for Robin.

The trip was awkward, with Amelia sullenly leaning against the window, until they got to a quiet area and again Robin insisted Beatty drive another time. They made Amelia swear to secrecy and not tell the adults. Beatty was still nervous, only this time she could feel the clutch gripping and didn't kangaroo hop nearly as much, just a few Joey hops. The atmosphere changed and the day became more of a fun outing than work, but clouded by the dark thought of Joyce's disapproval of Robin and the devastating blow to his male pride by failing in his responsibility.

They worked solidly, lifting the heavy boxes onto the truck tray. When they stopped for lunch, Robin was ravenous but Beatty had no appetite, due to her upset. Amelia tucked in, and then had a little snooze on the blanket. She was proving to be as lax as Harry was as a chaperone but this time their consciences and the blanket of guilt demonstrated to be an overwhelmingly omniscient vigilante. Robin moved close to Beatty and kissed her, but knew he wouldn't let it go any further, despite his instincts that urged him on to steal her away to the derelict cottage for an impulsive but loving romp in the hay. He swallowed his impetuous thought.

"I've brought you something in case we can't see each other for a while." He pulled out a thick mauve envelope.

Beatty looked at him, biting her bottom lip to stop herself from crying. Inside was a poem that he'd written especially for her.

I feel like writing poetry when I'm with you,
But I never was a poet.

The wine I drink when I'm with you,
Was never contained in a vessel.

The perfume I smell when I'm with you,
Was never confined to a bottle.

The music I hear when I'm with you,
Was never made by an instrument.

The beauty I see when I'm with you,
Was never made by a human being.

The silk I touch when I'm with you,
Was never spun by a mulberry worm.

The Love I feel when I'm with you,
Overwhelms my body, mind and soul.

This Love never began,
But always was, eternal.
The infinite Love of the Divine.

Tears formed in Beatty's eyes, this was the most touching thing anyone had ever given her. She held it to her breast and knew she would cherish it forever.

Robin insisted Beatty drive most of the way home and she didn't mind as the concentration kept her over active mind off other things.

At one stage she said, "Robin, you say the 'love of the Divine', what do you mean by this 'Divine'?"

"Well, you see in my family we don't really believe in a 'God' as such, but we do believe in a powerful creative force full of Love, Peace and Compassion, this energy we call the 'Divine'." Robin explained.

"Sort of like substituting 'Divine' for 'God'?"

"Yeah, you could say that-whoa, slow down a bit, this is a sharp bend."

Amelia had her eyes closed, resting, so Robin put his hand on Beatty's leg and whispered, "Oh Bea, what we goanna do?"

"I don't know," she replied unable to even giggle at his attempt to cheer her up.

They arrived home physically and emotional exhausted.

"About time," said Amelia as she flounced inside.

"When can I see you, Beatty?" Robin asked as he held her hand.

"Oh, Robin, you heard what Mother said."

"I know but I can't wait forever . . . please."

"When I start back at the library, meet me there, then, ok?"

"All right, I sure will miss you, not a minute of any day will pass without me thinking of you."

Amelia burst out, "Come quick, Beatty, Evie is burning up with fever." Beatty dashed into the house, chaos greeted her, not the smell of Yorkshire pudding that she was expecting.

Evie was burning up with Scarlet Fever, she was whimpering in pain. Beatty knew it was all her fault as punishment for her sins. She had to get to confession otherwise Baby Evie would die. She had to get absolution for her sins. It couldn't wait til morning, she had to go now. She grabbed her shawl and stole out of the house.

She ran to their church and pounded on the door of the vicarage. Father O'Malley answered the urgent summons and found Beatty in a frenzied state of dishevelment. He listened to her fervent request to confess and opened up the old church. What he heard shocked him to high heavens.

Relieved but still troubled Beatty wandered home lost in her thoughts.

Mother chastised her for running off. She went in to visit Evie. The poor baby was running a dangerously high temperature, a vivid raised strawberry rash spread down her cheeks, throat, chest and abdomen. There was a white ring around her lips and eyes, flame red cheeks made her look like a sunburnt baby panda. Beatty's heart went out to her, she rocked her gently. Beatty stroked her soft baby curls, damp with sweat and hummed a tune to her. Evie looked at Beatty with pleading eyes, beseeching her to help take the pain away. She dipped a cloth into cool water and wiped her down. Mother and Gran hovered around, beside themselves. The three of them kept an all night vigil with Evie, doing whatever they could to relieve her pain.

The other children had all contracted it too, to lesser degrees and they complained of sore throats and ears along with the intense heat.

The night seemed to stretch forever. In the dimness, Beatty said, "Gee, Gran I hope you don't get it, or Mother."

"Well, dear, we are both very unlikely to; we've both had it when we were children, so we should have built up immunity. My only concern really is for Evie and the unborn babe." Gran whispered back.

Mother said, "I think you're getting muddled, Mummy, it's Chicken Pox which affects the unborn, I don't think Scarlet Fever does. Well, I best pray to the Virgin Mary to protect me, anyway."

In the middle of the night Beatty said, "We should get some of the bush herbs, Mrs Richardson said they helped her children."

"No, you know my feelings on that; I'll not have Abo quackery in my house." Joyce said wearily.

"But she has a point, anything if it helps, Joyce," Gran beseeched.

One of the twins cried out from the back room where they were installed in Gran's bed and as Beatty walked through the kitchen she pulled Gran aside and said, "Gran, we've got to do something, how about I go and find this healer?" Gran nodded her consent.

Beatty stealthily went out the backdoor into the night for the second time; she opened the co-joining gate and knocked on Mrs Parker's backdoor. She peered out the frosted glass and called out, "Who is it?"

"Just me, Mrs Parker, Beatty, I need to ask you something. It's very important." The door creaked open and Mrs Parker stood there stooped against the cool of the night air, her hair pulled tightly into curlers.

"I'm so sorry to wake you, but Evie is very sick, can you tell me where the Medicine woman lives?"

"Yes, dear, not to worry, she is in the reserve near the stream next to the church."

"Thank you . . . thank you so much, so sorry to wake you." Beatty hastily went along the back sanitary lane, hoping she wouldn't bump into the sanitary man doing his business.

She dashed to the reserve and called, "Kabbarli . . . Lena, are you here?" Through the trees she could see a small campfire so she crackled and stumbled her path over towards it. Kabbabli emerged from a small makeshift humpy made of bark and rusted corrugated tin. Beatty told her the news and with steady deliberation she mixed up the herbs.

When Beatty got back, Mother was dozing in an armchair with her feet up so she made up the tea, mixing in a liberal amount of honey and fed a bottle of it to Evie. Luckily Evie was so thirsty from the fever that she slurped it up and the effort of that brought blessed relief and sleep. She made a decoction for each of her siblings, urging them to drink the foul smelling brew and the whole house-hold fell into a quiet slumber.

When Beatty woke she couldn't believe she ached as badly as she did. Firstly, she thought it was from lifting the bees boxes, then she became aware of an intensely sore throat, a shiver ran through her body, and despite the fact that she was sweating and her sheets were damp she was extremely cold. She felt like she could barely open her eyes. "Gran," she mumbled, and instantly the older lady was beside her bed.

"Joyce, Beatty's come down with it too," she called out, then turning to her she whispered, "Bea, you did the right thing last night, all the other children have broken their fevers. That stuff helped, I'll make you some."

"Evie?" Beatty mumbled.

"Yes, dear, don't worry, Evie will be fine, she's pulled through. She'll be weak for a few days but ok, thank God." Gran straightened the crotchet rug over Beatty and went to make her tea. Beatty felt a dip in the side of the bed and Mother talking to her but she was too weary to hear, it was as if she was talking through water and to listen took too much effort, so Beatty dozed fitfully.

Troubling scenes and dreams played on a loop in her fevered brain. At one stage she was convinced she heard Gran say, "Evie didn't make it, the poor little mite has gone to heaven. Pull yourself together, child, we'll have to organise her funeral." Beatty felt under her pillow for the little fur koala that she had bought to give to Evie for Christmas, and sobbed into the peculiar smell of fresh leather. Weary from life and exhausted by the fever she felt like she was drowning and the whole world was a blur. In her agitated state she saw her Dad opening the letter from her explaining the loss of the bees and this was like a physical gun-shot and he doubled over in agony.

The sickness overtook her more than the other children because she was so stressed and rundown. As the days past she could hear the other children playing nearby, she even heard Amelia saying to Harry that school was open again, and they would be going tomorrow. In her fitful dreams she called out for Evie.

On the evening that her fever broke and though still exhausted she was aware of her surroundings, Mother brought Evie freshly bathed, ready for bed and tucked her in with Beatty. Beatty was so happy and relieved that tears filled her eyes and a sob choked her throat. She lifted up Evie's nightie, and buried her face in her soft tummy. Evie giggled, then climbed on top of Beatty, held her face in her chubby little hands and plastered sloppy but sweet kisses all over Beatty.

She then sat up in bed sipping a mug of warm broth to soothe her still inflamed throat and catching up on all the family news and community gossip. School was indeed back, their family was the last domino to fall down with the fever and Amelia said that Beatty had missed her exam. Mrs Richardson left a message that she missed Beatty at the library and to get in touch as soon as she was well. Robin was most concerned and dropped off flowers and chocolates. Mother had read to the children from 'A Secret Garden' when they got bored and to help them settle at night. Eight families they knew from church had lost children to the fever. Gran had completed Beatty's socks she was making for the soldiers. Life went on quite merrily without her she realised.

Laura bustles into Mrs Morton's room, "How are we?" she asks.

"Well, dear, I'm ok but I need a cold shower, I'm all hot and sweaty. My nightie is sticking to me."

"Ok," Laura said, "But it will have to be a quick one."

All fresh and clean feeling again, Laura helped her back into bed and handed her book to her, something fell out and fluttered to the ground, obviously it had been used as a book mark by a previous reader. In beautiful scrolled copperplate it read:

There are those that Write the Books,
And Those that Criticise Them.
Bea Meadows

Laura bent down and picked it up, read it and said, "How true." She passed it to Mrs Morton and continued, "Speaking of truth, Matron found out that Kristy planted the sharps in my bag, she has been reprimanded, given a ten day suspension and some stress counselling, then she'll probably be moved to another area."

"Well, good for you, dear." But no matter how much Mrs Morton searched the archives of her mind nor plumbed the depths of the memory cavern, she couldn't recall any incident, so she just let it slip.

Feeling better, Beatty sat up in bed and tried to compose two letters. One would be to the Headmaster explaining her absence and for permission to sit for her exam and another to Father to apologise for the loss of the bees. By far the harder of the two was the missive to her Father. When she thought of the heartbreak it would cause him, she could barely continue. She told him about the Scarlet Fever in a watercolour edition, not wanting to cause undue worry for him. She hardly knew what to say, she felt so distant and removed from him. She wrote about mundane home life thinking it would please him to hear of the antics of the children, not imagining it would create unbearable homesickness for him.

Matron rang to inform Jennifer of the changes at the Nursing home.

"I'm calling to let you know that your Mother won't be able to do a 'Runner' again. We've tightened up security and you'll need a new code to access her area. This place has been like an ant's nest with security guys all around installing the very latest technology."

"Oh, that is good news; I'll be able to sleep better at night. What about the enclosed court-yard area? That is one of her favourite escape sites." Jennifer wondered.

"Yes, that too requires a code. We are feeling quite proud of ourselves for our upgrade. I better keep working, bye for now." Matron hung up.

Jennifer was relieved but also slightly apprehensive, her Mother loved her freedom and wild sense of expression, it almost made her guilty to think of her unable to escape. Not that she needed the worry and drama that escape brought but she had promised a place which maintained her sense of dignity, self-respect and individuality. Well, she justified to herself, Mother would hardly know, she wasn't very with it any more.

CHAPTER
TEN

Beekeeper Blues

Beatty addressed the envelope to the Headmaster and told Harry to hand deliver it as soon as he arrived at school. Then she sank back into the bed. She felt so weary, as if she had been hit by a tram. It felt as if she would never fully wake up again. She dosed on and off all day. When she got up, she scraped the remaining porridge from the aluminium pot, drizzled some honey on the grey, unappealing, conglomerate mass and fed some to Evie and had a bowl herself. It was quiet with the other children at school and Mother and Gran catching up on chores. She snuggled back into bed with Evie and read her a story, before they knew it they were sleeping peacefully together. The women smiled down at them and gave thanks that they had survived.

When the children burst through the door in the afternoon, Beatty woke as if the sun shone directly on her face. She felt so much better. The headache that had blinded her for over a week had miraculously lifted and her head was clear.

Harry handed her a letter with official school letterhead. It read:

Dear Miss Beatrice May Fielding,

I regret to inform you that permission cannot be granted for you to sit for your Teacher's Certificate this year. Even late applications closed over a week ago. I do realise that you have extenuating circumstances due to your own and your family's ill health. Bearing this in mind I will inform my superior and ask that you be given permission to sit for your certificate at the end of next year. Since you have missed a lot of school this term, might I suggest you apply yourself more diligently in future.

I trust that this finds your health and that of your family greatly improved.

Yours Faithfully,
Headmaster Harold Rowbottom

Beatty rested her head in her in her trembling hands. How dare he? She was a good student, she always handed her work in on time, practiced her French, endlessly interspersing it in her life and wrote all her essays neatly. Yes, how dare he? She'd show them all. Tomorrow she'd get up early and go see Mrs. Richardson. But for now, she had some catching up to do. She called the children around and quizzed them on where they had gotten up to in the Secret Garden. They filled her in.

Rupert tilted his mischievous little face, "You couldn't read from where you left off could you? Mum doesn't do the voices real-like like you do, we miss Ben Weather-staff's quirky accent."

Beatty was chuffed and filled with renewed vigour, she read fluently and dramatically. Putting on her best animated Yorkshire accent, she made the children's faces light up with laughter.

Despite the fact that when she woke next morning, she felt like not only had she been hit by a tram but run over by it as well, she summoned all her reserves and resolved to get up and do all that she had thought of last evening. She walked to the Corner Store and chatted to Andy Brown, the proprietor, listening carefully to his broad accent and intonation so that she could reproduce it for the story reading later. She recalled her Father calling him 'The Village Idiot' on days when he seemed to blither around his store as if lost on the moors of his homeland, or 'The Village Thief' if he felt that his prices were day light robbery.

Beatty scanned the shelves for an iron tonic, and when she couldn't find one she reluctantly asked, "Do you stock iron tonics?" knowing full well the whole neighbourhood would know by the end of the day.

Andy scanned her up and down, "Oh, aye an' what would tha' be needing it for, thou art a strong young lass?"

"Oh, I just feel run down from the Scarlet Fever, I can't remember a time when I was ever this tired before. So, I need to strengthen up my blood."

Andy bent down behind the counter and brought up a dusty bottle of iron tonic, he wiped it on his apron and set it on the counter. Beatty felt slightly ashamed as if she was buying something illicit, "Tha'll be strong in no time with this. Also, there is a little package for thee."

Beatty went out with the tonic and the package of photographs hugged to her chest. She strolled down the street to the library, feeling that every step was mechanical and she just had to let her body robotically respond. Before she knew it she was at the library, where the automaton took over the dusting and polishing.

"Beatty, Beatrice, I've been trying to get your attention. Are you feeling alright? You look peaky and pale; perhaps you ought to go home and rest up." A concerned look crossed Mrs. Richardson's face.

The room spun around and suddenly all went black and Beatty crumpled in an unconscious mass.

Mrs. Richardson rushed to her and patted her cheeks, "Quick someone, get me some water."

A kind, elderly man sprung into action bringing a glass of water. He swiped some of it around her face.

"I feel sick," Beatty said.

"Quick get up to the lavatory then, dear." Mrs. Richardson helped her up.

The kind gentleman offered to take her home and Mrs. Richardson accepted on her behalf.

Another wave of nausea overwhelmed her on arriving home and she dashed through to the backyard dunny. She heaved until she felt hollow inside. She sat in the garden catching her breath and she remembered the photos so took them out and opened up the package. Her birthday flooded back. Father was smiling and she missed him so much, his easy camaraderie and jovial nature. She put the two photos with Robin in them aside as she knew Mother would probably burn them in the stove without a second glance. Despite Robin's remorse and considerate attention while Beatty was ill, Mother would not let go of the grudge she held.

Mother called out, "Beatty are you ok? Come in I'll make you a cup of tea to settle your stomach."

Beatty sat at the table with Mother and Gran cradling the cup of tea in her hands and took tentative sips. Noisily the daily post clonked to the wooden floor through the slot in the door.

Mother ambled along the hall to collect it. There was an official looking letter. A sense of dread gripped her as she torn open the envelope with a bread and butter knife. It simply stated: Charles

Rupert Fielding is recovering in an Australian Hospital Base from a serious injury. He will be shipped home as soon as possible.

Once again Beatty felt light headed and nauseous so rushed outside for some fresh air. She sat on the low garden wall near the dunny, breathing deeply trying to calm her emotions. The bees buzzed in the nearby borage plant, humming their busy melody as they worked the fresh little blue star flowers. Her mind wandered to Robin and how bad he felt with the loss of the bee business. How will she ever be able to send Father the letter, or face up to him especially now that he was seriously wounded. How terrible for him to return home to this loss. She wondered if he had lost a limb or been disfigured or worse if he had changed and was no longer the Father she grew up with and loved. She'd heard about the devastating affect war had on people's minds, some she'd heard went totally crazy. The sun beat down on her face and lulled her to sleep, slumped against the dunny wall.

She vividly dreams of seeds sprouting vigorously in the garden in a wild chaotic assortment, she wanders around barefoot, flitting about the garden like a butterfly breathing in the moist fragrant air, the scent of honeysuckle wafting on the breeze. She bends over and sucks the sweet nectar from the base of the flowers. Suddenly, her Mother approaches with a pair of large, rusty scissors. They squeak as she ruthlessly hacks off Beatty's beautiful thick, wavy, auburn hair, leaving her with short spiky tufts. Her Mother then tips strawberry jam over her head, the bees buzzing in the nearby blossom suddenly start swarming around her attracted to the sugary smell, they start crawling over her cheeks and down her neck, next they are stinging her face, it is unbearable, only that the skies suddenly burst forth with torrential rain and lightening vividly brightens the sky that she is saved, the bees dissipate.

She dashes to the outhouse for shelter. As she stands there, dripping wet, she looks down at herself, totally naked, her belly grows before her eyes, and it is filled with grotesques creatures. She knows that eventually she will have to give birth to them and look after them. She woke in a hot sweat.

She pottered around in the garden until she felt calmer, the children were playing happily and the adults had agreed not to trouble them with the news. As the shadows grew longer she packed up and went inside with an arm full of veggies. She felt very detached from the merry family scene but participated once again on automatic pilot.

The next day after work, Robin was sitting on the steps waiting for her. "Good afternoon, my beautiful Bea, how are you?"

"I'm getting better, but I'm still really tired, how are you?"

"Well, I'm healthy but I hate myself, that's why I came to tell you . . ."

"Tell me what, c'mon, don't keep me waiting?"

"C'mon, sit down. You know I truly feel bad about the bee business, don't you?" He said.

"Yes, of course I do, so what . . . ?" She asked.

"Well, I've decided I'll have to go off to war, I'm going to enlist, to do me bit for me country and prove that I'm a man, after all. I just can't cope knowing what I've done. This might in some small way make up for it, in a way, I know it doesn't really change anything but I will feel better." He started rambling on.

"Oh, no Robin, not you, too! We just got a letter, yesterday that Father is seriously wounded, don't go, Rob, I couldn't stand it."

"Listen, Bea, I have to go, can't you see. I can't live with myself like this. Nothing's going to happen to me, I promise. I'll be back before you know it. Please try to understand, sweetheart." They walked home in silence. When they got there Robin said, "I'll pick you up from the library tomorrow when you finish, ok?"

"Sure, that would be really nice." She walked inside in a daze; feeling so shell shocked by all the changes.

The next day after work, Robin was waiting as arranged, she climbing into the truck. "I'm so sorry to spring this on you; Darling, but I've booked you in for your driver's license test. What with me going away you'll need it and as none of the women in your family drive, you are the closest." Not Mother, Gran or Mrs. Brownell had ever had any inclination to learn.

"But, Robin, I can't I've had hardly any practice, I'm not very good," She argued.

"Don't worry, honey, they are making it easy for women what with all the men away at war, you'll be fine."

With so little time to build up nerves, Beatty steeled herself. As Robin had said the kindly old driving inspector was very lenient and understanding and he passed Beatty with a warning to practice on deserted country roads and in no time he assured her, she'd be proficient. He dropped her off and arranged to meet at the library again the next day, same time only this time would be the last before he left.

Beatty stayed up late working by the dim light, embroidering the handkerchief she was making for Robin.

The next day dragged and she couldn't wait to see him. She whisked through her chores at the library, not lingering but ultra efficient, she just hoped that Mrs. Richardson didn't look too closely. When Robin tapped on the door, Beatty let him in locking it behind him and led him through to a secluded corner near the cleaning supplies closet. She gave him the socks she had been making which Gran finished off and the handkerchief. He ran his fingers over the embroidered 'R', and the little flame breasted Robin and superb blue Wren, "Oh, Bea this is beautiful, I shall treasure this and always keep it in my breast pocket close to my heart, thank you." He leant over and kissed her. He gave her a gift too, a simple oval, silver locket on a chain and another envelope with a poem in it.

"It's called a 'Sweetheart locket', look I've had it engraved for you." She turned it over and ran her finger over the scrolled engraving,

To My Honey Bea, Love Always,
Your Robin

He put it around her neck, lifting back her hair and kissing her at the nape of her neck sending delicious tingles through her whole body. She held the envelope and was about to open it. "Don't read it now," he said, kissing her and cupping her breasts. She threw her arms around him and enthusiastically showed him how much she'd miss him. They ended up on the floor of the cleaning closet saying goodbye with their bodies. They made passionate love with abandon and when they were breathless and spent they lay together in each other's arms. Beatty rested her head on Robin's chest listening to the racing beat of his heart and felt an overwhelming gush of love for him. This heart belonged to the most precious beautiful person in her world. They floated in a daze of swirling rainbows. She knew she'd be home late and would get in an awful barney with Mother but it was worth it, every precious moment was golden. When she finally said 'goodbye' to Robin she couldn't hold back the tears. She wiped her eyes and went in preparing for the attack, but when Mother saw how upset Beatty looked she left her alone. She crawled under her eiderdown quilt and read the parting poem Robin had given her.

I vividly dream I am entwined with you,
And wake beside you enjoying spring's balmy breath,
But it is nothing compared to the sweet honey of your lips.

Our feet sink into the lush dewy grass cushioning us softly,
While the sun glistens on dewdrops in their clover cups.
Rainbows arch around us and the flower carpeted
meadow looks
Bejeweled.
Sweet nectar of ideas is humming in the beehive of your
brain,
You share them and like the bees we dance then roll
around in
Laughter.
We are the Apple Isle Honeymooners.
Deeply infused with the intoxicating Bliss of Love.

And I do Love You, Bea, and I always will, Your
Robin XO

She curled up under the comforting feathers, making a little nurturing nest and cried herself to sleep.

The thunder rumbled, dark inky-grey clouds loomed overhead and the lights flickered until they went out totally. Mrs. Morton rested her book on the bed and went to see what was going on. Lightning flashed and lit her way. She wasn't scared, far from it. She loved the excitement and electricity in the air. She wandered along the corridor and in the dimness she tried the handle on the door to the outside world. To her surprise, it opened. Their new high tech super duper security system needed power to operate. She breathed in the crisp air and felt exhilarated and in her elation she floated out the door into the impending down pour.

CHAPTER
ELEVEN

The Taste of Freedom

Her feet sink into the cushiony grass and the earth squishes up between her toes. She whirls around in delight arms outstretched. As she walks along the path the gravel pokes into her feet, making her hop and skip a bit. She bends into people's front gardens smelling the roses. She lifts her face to the balmy spring air, thick with potential; the first heavy drops of rain seem suspended, gathering courage. Suddenly, the sky opens and a torrential downpour obscures vision. The driving rain has penetrated her dressing gown and is running down her neck in little rivulets, her hair is plastered to her head, yet she felt so good, so alive. Curtains fluttered as people looked out at the down pour. She, however nonchalantly wandered along, oblivious to the obvious spectacle she created.

She bent to pick up a little round stone, stroking its smooth surface instinctively knowing it would bring her peace. The owner of a café was standing in the doorway watching the downpour and invited her in for a cuppa. Inside was warm and dry, with a cheery, homely setting. He brought her a towel and directed a little fan heater towards her. When he asked her if she would like a cuppa she replied that she was sorry, she seemed to have forgotten her purse. He reassured her it didn't matter. She brought out an assortment of lint covered items from her pocket. Fifty cents, a pen, a choc éclair candy only half in it's wrapper, he insisted it was on the house, after all it wasn't every day in this semi-parched country of theirs that they had rain like today's, so they may as well celebrate. She picked the fluff off the candy and sucked on it while she was waiting for her tea. The pen still worked and she drew on the menu and serviette. Rain had the ability to open up the channels of creativity for her, she felt fresh, bright and renewed.

He brought the cup of tea and a scone and strawberry jam. He pulled out the chair opposite, leant back with his arms stretched back; hands clasped behind his head and started to quiz her.

"What is your name? Where do you live? . . ."

She shook her head. She didn't feel like being interrogated but nor was she quick enough off the mark to fabricate a new name and life for herself in a split second as much as she'd like to still be able to do so. She loved the freedom of the outside world. All she'd ever asked for was to die in her own home with dignity, her own web, that she had spun over her lifetime, with the hub of her worldwide supporters and admirers. Her nest, lined with feathers and safe from the attack of predators. She sipped her fragrant tea, it smelt like fresh hay and flower filled meadows not like the stale tea at the home and she bitterly resented those that had degraded her by institutionalising her.

The owner walked into the next room, the steady thrum of rain continued beating down on the roof. She felt cosy and her doodling was coming along nicely, very free and swirly.

"Hello there." She was startled out of her reverie and greeted by two dashing but drenched fresh faced policemen. "How are you today, get caught in the downpour, did you?" They enquired.

The nursing home had rung the police when they noticed Mrs. Morton's absence and their own security guy couldn't find her. The café owner had rung in to inform them of her arrival and it was fairly easy to match the pieces of the jigsaw together. They hadn't however anticipated that a sweet little bedraggled old lady would put up such a fuss.

"No, I won't go anywhere; I want to stay here with my son. Don't send me away again." She raised her voice. "I haven't done anything wrong, I just want my freedom. I'll not ride in a police car like a criminal. It's not a crime to enjoy a cuppa, is it? I've tasted freedom in my tea; I'll not give it up again."

"It'll be alright, come along, don't make a scene." One of the policemen tried to support her under the arm to help her out to the car. She elbowed him in the stomach. "By crikey, you're a vicious old lady, aren't you?" he said, doubling over. She kicked and screamed, lashing out but they didn't want to be rough with her in case they broke her bones. The owner suggested they call the Nursing Home and have them send someone she knew down to collect her, in the Nursing home bus.

The Nursing home had rung Jennifer when they found her Mother missing and she had gone there in a frenzy, not waiting to hear if she had been located yet. When she arrived, Matron apologised, excusing the security system and blaming it on the power failure, when the power failed, in case of fire the security automatically unlocked, a sort of safety feature she justified. She told her they had found Mother but that she wasn't cooperating and an orderly was going to go down and would she please accompany him.

They drove along the picturesque suburb and Jennifer was amazed at how far her Mother had wandered.

Mrs. Morton was still overwrought when they arrived and immediately started accusing Jennifer of being the main warden of the prison she had escaped from. The orderly talked to her in a low mellow tone, wrapped his arms around her and lead her to the bus. Violent shivers shuddered through her body as they drove back and put the fan on high to warm her.

Back at the home, clean and dry and duly chastised, Mrs. Morton sat propped up by pillows in her bed and continued reading from where the book fell open, on its own accord.

Christmas this year didn't feel like Christmas at all, but despite her general malaise, Beatty made an effort for the children, as she was sure Mother and Gran were doing, too. Everyone dressed for church and Beatty surprised everyone by offering to drive them in turns in the truck and with a flourish she produced and unfolded her license. A smirk spread over her face to see the varying reactions. Mother frowned, unsure. Gran's eyes twinkled with pride. Harry said, "How'd ya manage that, Roo. Cor, you can teach me now!" Amelia was amazed. Gregory and Rupert were chuffed; they thought the world of her anyway. And little Evie patted her hand and said, "Dood dirl!" It would be three trips but it was good novelty value.

The service dragged for all the family but especially the children who couldn't wait to get home to unwrap the few parcels that were scattered around under the branch they had as a tree. It was simple but cheerful with tinsel draped around and home baked biscuits hanging in it, there was a tinge of sadness and Beatty thought of how all three men who were important and integral to her life were away at war, Father had always said things travelled in threes. Perhaps this was now the start of three good things. Christmas was very simple this year but it looked fancy through the eyes of the younger children who couldn't clearly remember previous Christmases.

She ferried the family back home and the women found it rather nerve wracking. In the back yard she got Harry to help her grub tiny 'tatters', new season potatoes, and carrots for the baked dinner. She explained that he is now the man about the house, with Dad away and that he has to help out more, she was sure he was old enough to get a job. They scrubbed the veggies and put them in to cook while they went to share their gifts.

Beatty enjoyed the reaction of pleasure that she got from everyone for the gifts she gave them. Mother and Gran loved their embroidered handkerchiefs and wondered where in the world she'd found the time for such beautiful intricate stitching. She'd bought a jar of cold crème for Amelia, from the corner store, and Amelia was very pleased to receive such a grown up gift. The boys cheered at their marbles and immediately wanted to play a game, skiting that they would each have the biggest collection of all, the local lads would be green with envy. Evie immediately cuddled her koala then threw her arms around Beatty and kissed her saying, "Tank woo, Bea."

After lunch, Beatty was drying up and putting away along aside her Mother when Mother said, "I don't want to know how you managed it, Beatty, but I want to thank you for making such an effort to make Christmas special for the little ones. Without you it would have been nothing."

She smiled at her and before they knew it they were sharing a rare hug and a few tears. "I appreciate you, too Mum, I know it is hard on you with Dad away, and the worry of that. You are a remarkable woman. Thank you for everything."

When the library opened again after the Festive season, Beatty could barely look at Mrs. Richardson, thinking she would be able to read her like a book and that she would know exactly what had happened in the cleaning closet. With extra gusto Beatty cleaned to perfection. The toilet and hand basin had a gleam like they'd never had before and the wooden tables were so highly polished they reflected the shelves and the patrons. Beatty looked at her own reflection and thought she was looking prettier somehow.

CHAPTER
TWELVE

Betrayed

Beatty woke and immediately felt the bile rise in her throat. She dashed through the kitchen where her Mother was huddled in front of the open door of the stove, the fire flickered and threw an eerie glow on her face, and her hands nervously fingered her rosary as she mouthed her morning prayer. She looked up, startled as Beatty rushed through to the dunny. Beatty had just burst into the garden when her stomach heaved and emptied its sour contents all over a calendula plant. Mother came to hold her hair back as she retched and vomited violently again. When it seemed the internal storm had past, she wiped her mouth and it occurred to her that she was making a disgustingly bad habit of this excursion on arising. She really had been knocked about by the Scarlet Fever. She thought she ought to go to the doctor to make sure everything was ok.

She dressed for work and as she tied on her worn but still sturdy brown leather boots she decided she would go as soon as she finished her morning rounds of dusting and polishing at the library. She felt puzzled that the iron tonic hadn't made one iota of improvement despite the fact that she had been having a spoonful of the acrid decoction twice a day. She'd stashed the bottle down beside her mattress along with a spoon. Because she had arranged a last minute appointment, she had a long wait to see the doctor. She half heartedly flicked through a magazine.

The doctor greeted her by name having treated her and her family since before she was born, he ordered her up on the treatment table, felt her abdomen and asked her questions about the Scarlet Fever, then much to her horror he asked, "And where are you in your menses cycle?" His eyes twinkled in his weather beaten face.

"Pardon?" she asked shaking her head, unsure she had heard the question right.

"You know, when was the last time you had a visit from 'Aunty Flo', or 'Aunty Rose', your monthly time?"

"Oh, that!" and Beatty blushed beetroot red, "well, it has been a while I suppose, I lost track, what with being sick and all."

"Just as I thought, Beatrice, you are pregnant," her brow knitted with bewilderment, "That's right, you are expecting a baby."

"But, but, I can't be, how did that happen?" she stammered.

"Well, dear, you must know better than I do."

"But Robin said it wouldn't happen the first time!"

"Unfortunately, that piece of information, often taken as gospel is an old wives' tale, it can happen and did, you are living proof of it."

Beatty blanched and was pleased to be sitting down as the all too familiar light-headedness was threatening to consume her again.

"Where is the father of the baby? Gone to war?"

Beatty nodded through her tears. How was she ever going to live down the shame of this?

"Please don't tell anyone, especially don't tell my Mother, will you?" She half choked.

"No of course not, I'll keep your confidence but you will have to tell your Mother, and soon. Be strong." All she could do was nod, not trusting herself to speak again.

She wandered aimlessly along the footpath, tears streaming down her face but her feet purposely took her to the library. She asked Mrs. Richardson for some paper and a pencil. She sat in a secluded corner and composed a letter to Robin.

My Dearest Robin, you cannot begin to fathom the depth that I miss you. I feel like barely a drop of water in the bottom of an almost dried up well. It has been very hard just making an effort to get up every morning. This is difficult to say but because I haven't felt well since the Scarlet Fever, I went to the Doctor. He was very nice but he thinks you left me with a parting gift and that I am expecting. That's right I'm carrying your baby, darling. As yet I am still reeling in shock, but it is so nice to know that I carry your life in mine. How is the war? Is it so very dreadful, darling? Do you miss me? I wish we had gotten married before you left. I don't know how Mother and Gran will take this news. (I'm not sure if I should even keep it, the family relies on me to work. Unsure if this was the right thing to say she hastily crossed it out, thinking it would cause him guilt and anxiety.*) I dare say it will be a shock to them, too. I trust you are well,*

Robin dear.

With my Love and kisses, Bea.

She unclipped the latch on the locket she had worn around her neck since he gave it to her and looked down into the photo of Robin nestled within, standing nearby her on her sixteenth birthday. She smiled sweetly with the fond memories. She folded the letter, and put it in her handbag and made her way home. She wasn't due to clean at the library for many hours, yet. She sat on her bed and surreptitiously addressed an envelope for Robin Brownell, c/—The Royal Australian Army, and the headquarters from where they made every effort to deliver to the soldiers where-ever they were and then she intercepted Harry after school, on his way to play marbles, with a bribe of the promise of boiled lollies and orders to deliver the letter to the store immediately in time to meet today's post. She sank on her bed and the weariness of the day overcame her and she fell into a dreamless sleep.

She woke with a start and hastily prepared to go to work. She bustled along the street and just arrived at the library as Mrs. Richardson was locking up for the day. "You're terribly late, Beatrice, I'm very disappointed in you. You better have a good excuse." She said.

"Not really, I was tired and had a rest and slept a bit long, no one woke me because they thought I needed the sleep. I've been awfully tired lately."

"Perhaps you need a few days off?" She asked sympathetically.

"No, no, its fine, I can manage." Beatty knew the family needed and relied on the financial supplementation now that the bee business had collapsed. It was sweet relief to work at the library openly without having to hide the fact anymore. Her job was reluctantly accepted because the extra money was welcome.

She resolutely cleaned the toilet and floors, distractedly allowing her body to perform her duties while her mind was racing along, unsure of her next step. She considered seeing if Kabbarli Lena might be able to help her commit the ultimate sin in her restricted Catholic religion, abortion. She really didn't know what was involved she just knew it was a terrible thing to do, essentially an act of murder. She'd heard of an unfortunate girl at school who had gotten herself drunk then plunged a knitting needle up inside her, thus inducing a miscarriage and then there was her vague disappearance, explained by some that she had gone crazy and that she'd been taken off to a lunatic asylum. Beatty's mind wandered and she wondered what Robin's 'Divine' would have to say. She also wondered if the medicine woman would approve or even assist her in the shameful act she was considering; didn't the Aborigines also revere life as sacred? She didn't know if she could go through with it, but at least it would save her skin from her Mother and Gran. She locked up with the solid familiar, reassuring clonk and furtively looked over her shoulder and down the street to see if anyone was about. She started walking towards the Aboriginal medicine woman's bark humpy but part way there, she lost her nerve and instead found herself knocking on Robin's Mum's door.

"Beatty, what a lovely surprise, do come in."

"Thank you, Mavis."

"Are you alright, dear? Come in and take a seat." She led her through the narrow hallway to the ottoman couch. "Can I get you a cup of tea?"

"Yes, please that would be lovely." Beatty said and perched on the edge and tried to compose herself. Perhaps Mavis would know what she should do. Now was her chance to find out the 'Divine's' view on deliberate termination.

They chatted but Beatty didn't gather the courage to raise the one topic foremost in her mind . . . her unexpected pregnancy. Neither had heard from any of the three men yet, but Mavis promised that she would come around as soon as she had word. Heaven knows she'd enjoy the outing. She certainly felt lonely in this house all by herself. Beatty half envied her the quiet and solitude.

On the walk home Beatty impulsively decided that she wouldn't mention it to anyone until her mind was made up and she felt stronger.

As she opened the front door she heard her Mother holler, "Beatrice May come here immediately!" Dread filled her; she knew that tone of voice.

The three women, Mother, Gran and Mrs. Parker from next door sat around the table. Her stomach turned at the cold reception she received. Mother looked at her in disgust as if she was a built up soap scum ring in the laundry trough, then Beatty searched Gran's face and Gran looked at her as if she was something unwelcome growing in her face cream. She screwed up her face and looked away. In the middle of the table was Beatty's letter to Robin, looking the worst for wear. Mother pushed the crinkly letter along the table towards Beatty, "So, is it true?"

A lump rose in Beatty's throat, she nodded.

"By jingo, I really will tan that Robin boy's hide when he returns from war!" exclaimed Gran.

"You may as well know, we are highly disappointed in you, Beatrice May." Mother added. This was the second time today that Beatty had been told this.

"I would have thought more of you than this," chimed in Mrs. Parker. Beatty turned to flee to her bed but Mother said in a stern voice, "Don't you dare turn your back on me young lady, I'm not finished yet. You're Father and I had such hopes for you, now you're facing Eternal Damnation. Not only have you lost your virginity you've also been entertaining mortal sin, oh yes, we read what you had crossed out. I won't have it; you will have this baby and suffer the consequences." Beatty dashed to her room as sobs choked her throat.

She lay in bed, with, 'Be ye sure your sins will find you out,' repeating itself in her head stuck on a torturous loop.

Suddenly she thought, 'Drat that Harry, he's in for it when I see him.' It didn't take a brain surgeon to piece together the sequence of events. Obviously, Harry had abandoned the letter on the footpath as he played marbles, and totally forgotten it. Mrs. Parker had picked up the damp missive and carefully dried it out over her stove then much to her delight read the faded pencil scrawling, Beatty's note of admission to Robin and delivered the scandalous news first hand. Mrs. Parker was the very live wire of the bush telegraph itself, it would be all through their little suburb in no time.

Beatty had to get out; she grabbed her shawl and made a hasty but stealthy retreat. For the second time that day she found herself in front of Robin's Mum's house. She urgently knocked and Mavis called out, "Who is it?"

Beatty replied, "It's me Beatty, again. Mavis, I absolutely have to talk to you."

Mavis opened the door, tying her dressing gown tighter around her waist, "Whatever is the matter, Bea, come in and tell me." And Beatty blurted out the news.

Mavis put her arms around Beatty and consoled her. She reassured Beatty that Robin loved her and would marry her when he returns and that he would welcome a baby. Anytime that she needed to talk she could go there. Secretly Mavis was chuffed at the prospect of a grandchild, for too long now apart from her role as a homemaker and her handcrafts she'd felt that her life held no particular purpose. They shared sweet tea; the all round panacea, then Beatty went home to bed feeling stronger and more positive. She slept fitfully with vague unsettling dreams.

Just as Beatty was waking next morning she heard a tremendous crash and a scream followed by a low moan. She raced out to the hall. There was her Mother lying curled in a foetal position amongst ceramic shards. "Mother, are you hurt?" She lay there mentally assessing the injuries. "Oh Bea," she moaned, "I have such a stabbing pain in my lower back and abdomen."

"Don't worry Mother, I'll send Harry out for the doctor." The loud commotion had woken everyone in the household and they all gathered around.

"She won't lose the baby will she Gran?" Amelia asked.

"I don't know yet, dear, we'll have to see what the doctor says. Joyce, are you bleeding?"

"No, but I feel all wet, I think me waters broke."

"Wow, Mum, how did it happen n how many steps did you slip down?" Gregory asked wide-eyed.

"You're in trouble boys because I slipped on a marble," she replied, then muttered under her breath, "Bother that Beatty for giving the boys marbles for Christmas." Not 'bother the boys for leaving the marbles lying around' but she felt Beatty was to blame. Beatty could just imagine her Mother heavily pregnant ambling down the stairs, leaning on the banister for support when she trod on an errant marble and much to everyone's horror her legs flew out from under her and she crashed to the bottom, knocking over a vase which was a cherished wedding present and being in so much pain that it damaged her pregnancy and she went into premature labour and the baby was stillbo . . . . she shook her head trying not to entertain imaginary demons. She consciously checked her thoughts.

"Can you move, Joyce?" Gran asked.

Amidst lots of groaning with Gran and Beatty on either side of her, she was able to get up and hobble to Gran's bed to wait for the doctor. "Amelia, perhaps you could make yourself useful by cleaning up the broken vase." Beatty said as they passed her looking lost.

Gran and Beatty bustled around the kitchen, stoking the stove and preparing tea and breakfast.

By the time Harry finally arrived back with the doctor, the household smelled warm and inviting. Beatty checked the time, she would be late for work but surely Mrs. Richardson would understand and accept this as a valid explanation.

When the doctor emerged from behind the grey woollen blanket his face looked grim as he said, "Well, the good news is she is ok, a bit shaken up, the baby is still alive and has a strong heartbeat but the bad news is that unfortunately she has developed a hind water leak. Sometimes that can lead to premature labour and the baby is almost certainly too young to survive, but sometimes a hind water leak can seal itself up. She needs total bed rest for a least a week, then only light duties after that."

Gran looked at Beatty and said, "I dare say we'll manage."

"I've given her a shot of morphine and she should sleep for a few hours, Beatty, see me to the door . . ."

"Yes, sir." Beatty led him along the hallway where Amelia was bent down sweeping up the shards. At the door he said, "How are you today?"

"I'm much better, apart from concern for Mother, they know about my condition, it leaked out last night."

"Well, I think it is for the best. Don't go lifting anything heavy."

"No, I'll try not to, thank you for everything." She said as she quietly shut the door behind him.

Saturday arrived with blessed relief; it was the one day that Beatty could lie in bed for a little while. As she came up through the layers of sleep she allowed herself a delicious doze, her tummy felt surprisingly good, she hoped she was over the worst of it. Evie woke and Beatty climbed out of bed, scooped her toasty warm body up and took her back to her bed for cuddles. They played pat-a-cake and other soft games until the uriniferous stench from the overnight napkin became too much for Beatty and she got up to change Evie and get the porridge started for breakfast.

Mother was still in a lot of pain and as they couldn't afford for the doctor to come too often, Beatty suggested to Gran that they send Harry to fetch the medicine woman but Mother heard them from the behind the blanket curtain and called out, "No Koori quack will lay hands on me or any of my family for that matter." They exchanged glances knowing how indebted they were to the medicine woman for the fever herbs. So, instead Beatty decided to be resourceful and do what she could. She looked through an old herbal medicine book and found a recipe for a cream for bruising and thought she would give it a go with whatever ingredients they had available. From the garden she picked arnica, comfrey, lavender and calendula leaves and flowers. These she infused. Beating the dark fluid together with honey and melted beeswax a beautiful wholesome fragrance filled the air. She rubbed some on Mother's lower back and legs and the cramping eased and she was able to sink into a peaceful sleep. Everyone in the family was impressed with Beatty's new cream and it proved to be broadly useful for all number of ails. It was gentle enough for a bottom cream for Evie, and good for scrapes and bruises for the boys.

Beatty spent the rest of the day fulfilling domestic chores and ironing all the children's best clothes ready for church because she knew it would be expected of her to take them to the service in the morning.

When she woke she felt tired and longed to stay in bed but instead reluctantly dragged herself out to do her duty to her Mother and God. The little children were uncooperative and Gran said she'd stay to care for Mother, so Beatty had to battle with her contrary siblings. They were dressed in their best and did a procession past Mother's bedside for her approval. She nodded and they set off. Beatty had thoughts of truancy as they walked militarily in the warm summer sunshine, daydreaming of beaches and picnics whilst destined for a hard wooden pew in a cool uninviting building. They filed into their usual pew and sat as quietly as possible. The twins shuffled around and whispered and Beatty thought how Mother did a good job to control them all without words, then she employed the stern, 'Don't you dare disobey me,' look and the boys settled momentarily. All the church ladies were whispering and glancing around at Beatty. The news had spread like wildfire. Obviously her news had been a hot item on the bush telegraph last night. One church lady was covertly nominated while all the others kept their heads down, only sneaking furtive glances, and she approached Beatty and whispered fiercely, little globules of spit flying out under her lightly moustached top lip as she vehemently declared, "You're not welcome here, girl. You'll drag us all down into the eternal damnation with you. We won't have the likes of you taking communion alongside us. You should be ashamed of yourself, girl, and barely sixteen!"

Beatty got out her handkerchief and wiped her face. She then balanced Evie on her hip, grabbed Gregory by the hand and said, "C'mon children, we don't have to stay in this unchristian place." She walked briskly with her head held high down the aisle just as the priest was entering. The younger children had to jog to keep up. They kept a cracking place until they came to the edge of the bushland where Kabbarli had her temporary dwelling.

Beatty called and she crawled out from her humpy and greeted them warmly with a ready smile, flashing her red mouth and few teeth and they all sat around the fire, sharing tea from a chipped enamel cup and a crusty freshly baked damper, which they had to brush the ashes off. Kabbarli loved children and they liked her after the initial gaping in awe and she made them feel welcome around her camp fire and told them all lots of her tales of adventure as a medicine woman and midwife as she balanced Evie on her knobbly knees. They sat wrapped in intrigue. Evie rubbed Kabbarli's face thinking she was covered in a layer of dirt.

She talked of her people's history and how the white people had done an unscrupulous deal with her people to 'buy' the Port Phillip district, all 600,000 acres of it, to make Melbourne, Australia's most sprawling city, with the exchange of tomahawks, blankets, knives, mirrors, flour and other such inconsequential items. No wonder her people felt violated and displaced. Their land had been stolen along with their children and never had they been recognised as having any legal title to their own tribal lands. Such a shame. The older children listened in rapture never having heard this side of the story, ever before. They felt a strong sympathy for this woman with a heart of gold, living simply close to nature. Beatty knew she helped lots of white people but wondered how she could bare to deign to have anything to do with them after all they had put her peoples through.

Beatty told her about being shunned at church and found her to be an understanding, sympathetic listener. As they left, they promised to visit again. Beatty brushed everyone down but still they all looked really dusty and dirty. While they walked home she instructed everyone not to tell Mother or Gran about what happened at church as it would cause them undue worry and concern, it would be their little secret and as a reward Beatty would read extra from The Secret Garden, and as a bonus if no one mentioned church or Kabbarli at all, she would buy some boiled lollies later in the week. Dusty, dirty angelic smiles and nods assured her that everyone was going to diligently try to keep the secret.

As they entered the little terrace house Beatty heard the low timbre of a man's voice, her heart did a summersault, and then just as quickly it sank as she recognised Father O'Malley sitting talking to Gran.

Mrs. Morton's eyes were growing heavy so she put down the book, losing her spot.

CHAPTER
THIRTEEN

Patched Dreams

After her snooze, Mrs. Morton picked up her book and saw there was no book mark in it so let it fall open wherever and continued reading.

It dawned a hot hazy bushfire sort of day in early March, the sort of day to get your chores done early before you wilted completely. Beatty's cotton nightie stuck to her damp skin showing her protruding lower abdomen and fuller breasts as she made her way through the kitchen. She greeted the chooks and lifted her arms up to catch a breeze. An eerie sense of foreboding sent a shiver along her spine. Beatty collected the grey water saved from yesterday to water the wilting vegetable plants. Harry came out to go to the dunny and Beatty cornered him and nagged like a broken record, "You really are such a lazy kid. You can't even be trusted with a letter. You really ought to get a job, Harry; the responsibility would help you grow up. It's time you became the man about the house and helped us ladies out more."

"Sure, n what would I do? I'm too young for much."

"Ask Mr. Brown from the corner store, he might have a job for you. In the meantime, help me with this water, will ya, I'm dying in this heat. It wouldn't hurt for you to take over feeding the chooks, either."

When Beatty went back inside, Mother was slumped in one chair, her large pregnant tummy looking overwhelmingly full, with her swollen legs out stretched on another kitchen chair. "Thank God I've got less than a month to go," she sighed, "this has been my hardest confinement; yet, I suppose it's my age. The doctor did warn me when I had Evie that it wouldn't get any easier."

Beatty gave her a weak smile. She heard the familiar rattle and flutter of a letter being delivered so she bustled to collect it. To her surprise it was a letter from Robin. She quietly went to her bed to read it in private.

Dearest Beatty,

I search the crowd of thousands for your face alone, I'm weary yet I would walk to the ends of the earth to be with you, darling. Pity we are separated by a large expanse of water and I don't swim well.

The monsoon is merciless,
Here in this relentless rain,
I am obsessed by you,
You are my strength,
My courage, my will to live.

The war came too close today,
The birds stopped singing,
The crickets stopped chirping,
My heart stopped beating.

There was a deafening rush in my ears,
I held my breath and thought of you,
And only you.
With the air rushing back into my lungs,
I knew you are like oxygen to me.

I can't live without you, Bea and can't wait to be back
with you when this sodding war is done, darling, we will
be reunited. I love the socks you made me they are my
favourites but they stink so get clicking and clacking . . .
I love you, Darling Honey Bea and always will,
Your Robin

Beatty savoured the letter, hugging it to her heart, tears sprung to her eyes, she curled up on her bed and drowned her sobs in her pillow, she couldn't let on to Mother or Gran that she'd had word. She tucked the letter into her bodice as she dressed for work. She knew she would be awfully late again and that it jeopardised her chances of taking on more librarian work instead of just cleaning. She thought about what a mess she had made of her life just recently.

As she was polishing the counter, Harry arrived looking tousled and signalled for her to come over. She glanced over at Mrs. Richardson who was in a hushed conversation with a patron so she went over to him and said, "What is it Harry? Be quick."

"Come home quickly when you finish 'cos there is a trunk delivered and Mother says we shan't open it 'til you get back. Also, Mr. Brown says I can do a morning paper round and deliver some groceries to the oldies in our suburb, triffic, eh? I got a job." He was shifting uncomfortably and holding his left hand.

"Yes, that's really terrific. What's the matter?"

"Don't mind me, I got in a little brawl and hurt my thumb, look at it." Beatty touched the swelling, "I reckon you got a sprain."

"Don't tell Mother, will you, 'cos I'll get in real strife." He pleaded.

"No, I'll fix it when I get home, pleased you got a job now go before I lose mine. Tell Mother I'll be home in three quarters of an hour . . . go, scat." Beatty hoped that having work and a purpose would sort out her little brother, give him a sense of pride.

A Christmas air of excitement greeted her with all the children bursting around, jumping up and down, and clapping their hands. Beatty felt like a popular actress, everyone was so excited she was home. They pulled her by the hands and gathered around the trunk. It was made of solid gleaming teak with brass handles and lock making it an exotic intriguing treasure chest. Beatty and Gran opened it as Mother and the children looked on. The lid creaked back and revealed an array of glistening fabrics and precious things peeking through their wrappers. Everyone started to rifle through the yellowed newspaper looking at the ornate gifts. There were soft Kashmir shawls in beautiful colours for each of the girls and Gran, there was an Indian brass candle holder with mother of pearl inlay for Harry, a carved elephant with real ivory tusks and a statue of the three 'See no evil, hear no evil, speak no evil' monkeys for the twins but the 'piece de resistance' was a sumptuous quilt made from silks from saris and brocades shot with gold thread, this was obviously for Mother. An envelope with 'Joyce and Family' written on it fluttered out of some papers. Harry handed it to Mother. She cradled it then started to open it somewhat apprehensively.

My Dearest Family, Mother started reading aloud,

I know I am on my death bed and thinking of you all to the last. Here Mother developed a lump in her throat so she just mouthed the words but no sound came out, tears welled in her eyes. *I have a wound close to my HEART which has become gangrenous. I have arranged for Bob to take my recent wages and buy you all something to remember me by. I want you to know how much I love you all and will miss you dearly.*

Be strong for me, Joyce.
Your Loving Husband and Daddy,
Charles

Beatty grabbed the letter and Mother hurried out of the room. She clutched one of the shawls, a soft lavender coloured one close to her heart and shook as she read the letter. Another page fell out from behind it. It was written by Bob.

Dear, dear Joyce and Children, I am so, so sorry for your loss. Charles was a strong and brave man to the end.

My condolences, Uncle Bob Brownell.

The sparkles of the presents instantly lost their lustre. The room swam and Beatty could hear a rushing in her ears, she sank into the nearby armchair just as a hot faint stole her consciousness.

A nightmare woke Beatty, she saw her Father die of a heart attack as he read the letter about the collapse of the bee business. She woke flushed and breathless. 'Father can't be dead, not my own Daddy. He is indestructible, invincible.' She felt in a way it was her fault. She curled up in the armchair and wept.

Everyone tip-toed around the house lost in their own worlds of bereavement.

Evie needed tending to so Beatty reluctantly got up to prepare her mash and change her. Only the three younger children had any appetite. Despondently, Beatty did her duty.

As she slowly went about the kitchen chores she could hear her Mother sobbing fitfully on the other side of the grey blanket partition where she had been permanently installed in Gran's bed since she had her fall down the stairs. Every so often she let out a low moan.

"Are you in pain, Mum?" Beatty called out.

"Yes, you better call Gran."

Beatty went to the base of the stairs and hollered up, "Gran, Mum's in pain, you better come down."

She ducked behind the curtain.

"Beatty, I think it's me birthing pains started up."

"No, Mum it can't be, it's too early."

Gran emerged in the room and said, "Tell Harry to fetch the doctor, bring me some sheets and boil some water." Beatty stood there stunned. "For Heaven's sakes, child, get a wriggle on." Gran ordered.

She did as she was told and also served up some soup for the younger children and prepared a bottle for Evie.

The contractions increased in intensity. The groans and screams were starting to upset the children so Beatty told Amelia to look after everyone in the living room.

Harry came back, puffed and with a florid face, "He's not there, his housekeeper said he's away for a few days."

"Beatty go fetch the Abo," Gran ordered, "Your Mothers struggling!"

Harry cranked the truck and Beatty drove after a sputtering start to see if she could find Kabbarli. Luckily she was by her campfire and Beatty blurted out the news urgently. Kabbarli ducked into her humpy to grab a bag of supplies and they tore home.

Gran had prepared Mother for the arrival of the Medicine woman so she didn't kick up a fuss. She was in too much pain to protest. Anyone would be helpful, she felt so dreadful, so out of control but she momentarily thought that they may be a different colour on the outside but their internal workings are probably the same. She hoped so. A contraction overwhelmed her fleeting reasoning.

Mother started to fervently call to the saints and angels. "Holy angels of God, bless me, take away my pain. Blessed Virgin Mary come to me."

Kabbarli lit a bound stick of herbs and started smudging the labouring woman, "Be Dah, Be Dah," she chanted in a resonant drone as she waved the pungent smoke around. She pulled Gran aside, "She got very bad spirits around her. Dark evil spirit."

After a particularly strong contraction released its torturous grip, Mother started shouting hysterically and pointing to the curtain, "Get her out of here, she doesn't know what she is doing. That stuff stinks and I can't breathe."

"Perhaps you best wait in the kitchen," Gran whispered to Kabbarli. Gran went to her bedside, "Settle down, Joyce, everything will be ok."

"Beatty, bring me a basin of cool water and a face cloth."

Beatty entered the room, put the basin on the bedside table and rung out the cool water and placed the cloth on her Mother's forehead. She smiled down at her encouragingly trying to hide the overwhelming concern and the urge to flee that she felt.

Mrs. Morton stretched out her cramping limbs. She'd love a bath. She wandered down the corridor to find one of the carers to request one. She stood outside the staff tearoom and listened in to a conversation.

"I think I'll take a sickie tomorrow," one voice said, "I need a break from all these smelly, doddering oldies."

"Why don't you talk to Matron about getting a transfer, go and spend some time in the less secure area where they are easier to care for?" Another voice replied.

She tapped on the door, "Excuse me ladies, could you help me with a bath, I feel all hot and sticky?"

"Yes, certainly, Mrs. Morton." The carer put her arm through Mrs. Morton's and led her back to her room.

As the bath water ran in the carer added lavender oil and the fragrant steam filled the air and her soul making her feel comforted and relaxed. She soaked for as long as the carer could be patient, but even a shallow, business like bath was better than nothing. She supposed it was a bit of a bother as the carer helped her out into a towel, dried her down and slipped a nightie over her head.

Settled back in bed feeling fresh she remembered, 'That's right, the Mother was in labour, I wonder what happens next . . .' She found her spot and continued reading.

CHAPTER
FOURTEEN

A New Life

"Pant dear, don't push yet." Gran said. "Lena, get in here, she needs help."

Beatty was horrified by the excruciating pain her Mother was in. How could she bare it? She was restless and moving around on the bed. Kabbarli Lena said, "Get off your back, you are wasting your energy, try going on to all fours and letting nature help you." They helped her move, she was so weary, and she didn't think she could stand it any longer.

A contraction gripped her, she screamed. "Moo like a cow, woman, it is better to make low sounds," Kabbarli explained exasperated.

"Push now . . . and again," Kabbarli instructed.

Mother pushed and the baby's head crowned but retreated after the contraction.

"Big push, you baby want to come out, she very close now." Beatty was mesmerised, she couldn't believe she was witnessing this nor that she would have to go through it in a few months, herself.

Mother did as she was told, pushing with all her might. The baby's squashed face emerged.

"No push, pant . . . she got cord round her neck."

Kabbarli slipped the cord over the baby's head, "Now push," and the scrawny baby slipped into her hands, almost immediately the placenta fell out with a thud and a gush of blood.

With a cursory glance, eyes trained with years of practise Kabbarli noticed the cord was limp, the baby was still, she shoved it to Beatty saying, "Dis baby no good!"

She turned back to concentrate on the Mother as all good midwives are trained to do. She helped Gran flip her over, with every after birth contraction there was a huge gush of blood, they had to staunch the flow of blood or they would lose her, she'd haemorrhage to death. They had to work fast.

"Amelia, bring towels," Gran called, removing the sheets which were wringing wet with Mother's life blood.

Beatty looked down at the exquisitely perfect baby, momentarily she wondered how Kabbarli knew she was a girl before she was born, instinctively she blew on her face and held her up and smacked her bottom as she had read in a library book. The baby's back arched and she drew a breath and gave a thin but piercing cry. She drew another painfully bigger breath and continued crying. She was alive. Beatty grabbed a fresh towel and wrapped the tiny baby girl along with her placenta and held her close. Colour flooded into her tiny body.

Beatty walked to the side of the bed. Her Mother lay ghostly pale and lifeless. One body faded away as the other grew rosier. One body took its last shuddering breath as the other painfully fills its new lungs and secures a fragile grasp on life, hollering to clear the passage ways.

Gran and Kabbarli continued to work on Mother.

"Joyce, dear, don't leave us, think of the children, think of your new baby, c'mon, Joyce, fight for your life."

"Girl, bring me the stringy bark tea I made on stove," Kabbarli ordered Amelia who stood stunned in the corner.

She brought in the saucepan and the steam filled the air. Kabbarli mixed in some of the cold water from the bedside basin and soaked a towel in the infusion then wrapped it around Joyce, hoping its antiseptic qualities would help stop the pain and bleeding. Gran was still stroking Joyce's hair and pleading with her. The blood kept flowing and seeped into the new towel. Joyce's life blood had indeed flowed out unresponsive to the efforts of staunching applied by the two women.

"I so sorry, I think we lost her, she has slipped away to the dreamtime, nothing more we can do," Kabbarli said.

"Harry, go and fetch the priest," Gran called before she collapsed over her daughter's body in uncontrollable sobs.

Beatty sat with the baby by the fire, rocking her back and forth.

Kabbarli came and started to order the other children around. The twins were to make a small fire of wattle twigs in the back yard to smoke the evil spirits out of the infant. Amelia was instructed to bring dressmaking scissors. Beatty laid the infant on the well scrubbed kitchen table. Kabbarli felt along the cord until she came to a nodule and she cut through the cord with some effort at that spot. The infant had a raised hernia from her struggle with her tentative life and the old lady applied a waxy substance at the naval and bound the remaining umbilical cord stump and the protuberance with a rag around the baby's body. They cleaned the baby by rubbing in the excess vernix and wiping off any blood with a rag. They then took her little naked body outside to hold her over the smoke of the fire. They smoked her in the traditional ritual of the Aborigines, "She be good now," said Kabbarli. They took her in and Beatty sat rocking her to sleep.

Father O'Malley arrived with Harry and the focus shifted from the new life to the death of their beloved Mother. Beatty had been so tuned in to the baby it hadn't sunk in that Mother had died. Kabbarli felt uncomfortable with the religious ceremony and left saying she would check in tomorrow. They all stood around her bed as Father said the last rites. Then he said he'd send around some church ladies to help clean up and bring in some supplies. Gran climbed the stairs in shock and closed the door on her room. The children scattered to their beds and Beatty sobbed into the baby.

A few hours past and no-one showed up to help so Beatty bundled up the baby in flannelette cloths and put her down in a wicker laundry basket nearby and battled her grief and nausea at the iron rich stench of blood as she cleaned up. Soaking the towels and sheets in the laundry trough, she was too exhausted to scrub them today so they would just have to soak overnight. With a basin of warm water she sponged down the body of her Mother and applied her own sweet lavender cream. The hearse arrived and two elderly men quietly took Joyce away on a stretcher.

The baby woke and cried so Beatty heated up some milk and fed the poor little motherless mite. She'd actually fallen in love with her already totally mesmerised by her petite beauty. A gush of motherly love flowed through her as she watched her suckling and realised her total dependence on her. Gran had abandoned the baby in her grief; she hadn't so much as looked at her. Beatty knew she would be the mother to this little one without a blink.

Beatty held no illusions that the death of her Mother or her subsequent funeral would heal the rift in the church congregation, after all no-one had come to help or bring supplies. There was a very poor turnout at the funeral and she overheard a whispered conversation, "If you ask me that family deserves everything it gets." Tears flowed down Beatty's face onto the baby wrapped in a bundle in her arms. Surely, her family had now had their share of bad luck and the run of three, the loss of the bee business, the loss of Father and now the loss of Mother, could travel on and they deserved the blessings of three good lucks. Surely!

Beatty make a pot of soup and all the children sat around the kitchen table eating. Beatty said, "I guess we need to choose a name for the baby, what do you think?"

"Yeah, how about 'Devil' 'cos she took Mother's life?" said Harry.

"Harry, take that back, that's not nice, she is a sweet innocent baby. Mother went into premature labour from the shock of Father's death and she died of a massive haemorrhage. We are lucky at least that the baby survived." Beatty said.

"I know, how about 'Mary' because Mother called out to the Virgin Mary to help her, she liked that name." Amelia suggested.

"We could call her 'Babe'," said Rupert.

"Or 'Gertrude', that's my teacher's name," said Gregory.

"Bub, bub," piped in Evie.

"Shouldn't we call her 'Joyce' after Mother," said Harry, "or 'Florence' after Gran."

"No, I don't think so, it would upset Gran, and she's already taken it so hard that she can't look at the baby." Beatty explained.

Beatty looked down at the peacefully sleeping baby in her lap, "How about we call her 'Mary Eliza Lena'?"

Everyone agreed and a more jovial air filled the room. It was as if giving the new life a name they were embracing the future.

In the Nursing Home, Mrs. Morton pulled her soft mauve shawl around her shoulders and wandered down the corridor to go to the garden. The door was locked, she felt annoyed, she only wanted to see the stars and say, 'Good night' to the moon. She couldn't get out. She tried rattling the handle but to no avail. She shielded her eyes and gazed out and wondered what she did to end up here. She knew she had been a hardworking responsible person all her life. She didn't deserve this. Resentment crept in.

Jennifer decided to call in to check on her Mother on her way home from a meeting. As she passed the nurse's station she asked Matron, "How is Mother this evening?"

"Well, she is well, but she is restless and causing a bit of havoc, not sleeping much. You know how it is; she's up to the bit where the Mother dies in childbirth."

She walked briskly down the corridor and tapped lightly on the door, "Mother are you awake?" But there was no reply so she pushed open the door and looked around. Trying not to panic she thought of her Mum's favourite place, the courtyard, and walked quickly in that direction. As she rounded the corner she saw her leaning on the glass door peering out. She breathed a sigh of relief.

"C'mon Mother, come back to bed, you've only got a light cotton nightie on." She attempted to guide her back but she resisted.

"No, it's not fair. You've stolen everything from me, my youth, my golden years, my pretty dresses, my house, my garden. I can't stand you. Go away."

"Come now, Mother, you don't know what you are saying, you can't mean all that. I've only done what was best for you." She tried to link arms and support her back to bed. In her frustration Jennifer said, "C'mon Mum, or I'll call a nurse and they'll give you a dopey shot." The threat worked and she cooperated.

Mrs Morton continued to blame her daughter and after she got her settled she said, "Well, Mum if you are going to be in one of your moods, blaming me like this, I don't have to stay."

"Well, go then, you don't really care anyway. What's that you are stealing?"

Jennifer looked down at the dressing gown in her arms, "Mum, I was going to take it home to wash it, I'll bring it back next time I visit. If you treat me like this I mightn't visit again. Well, I just hope you are back to yourself soon. Bye for now."

"Old cow," she muttered as she walked back along the corridor, tears welling in her eyes. She tried to be understanding and compassionate but today her Mother's cutting remarks simply hurt.

Mrs. Morton started to straighten up her room. There seemed to be very few clothes hanging in the wardrobe and so many precious things seemed to be missing. She dusted her books with the sleeve of her nightie and remembered she'd been reading. She picked it up and resumed.

Beatty was overwhelmed by the way in which Gran seemed to be so detached and paralysed by her all consuming grief for her daughter. Beatty was now mother to a newborn baby, a two year old toddler, mischievous twin boys and Harry and Amelia as well as being pregnant herself. She really felt that she was forced into the role of matriarch prematurely. She made the correlation between herself and with the development of bees that were naturally thrust into adulthood in twenty-one days. Gran spent most of her days in her room at the top of the stairs only coming down for a bowl of soup occasionally. Sometimes Beatty got Amelia to take up a cup of tea.

Harry and Amelia had not gone back to school since Mother died. Beatty needed their help too much. Amelia walked the twins to school and stopped by the library to do Beatty's morning round of dusting and polishing on the way home. Mrs. Richardson was most sympathetic, but said she wouldn't tolerate slackness. If they slipped up she would sack them both. Beatty still went in the late afternoon to do the major cleaning and spruce up after Amelia.

It was a big task but to their credit both Amelia and Harry were for the most part rising to the challenge. Beatty made a point of saying, "Thank you for all your help. Mother and Father would both be proud of you." In order to encourage them to continue being helpful.

No-one gave her encouragement. No-one gave her compliments. No-one thanked her. She gathered that this is what it is like to be a mother and she was just getting an early taste of it.

CHAPTER
FIFTEEN

Life Goes On

Life was a continuous, blurry haze of chores and mouths to feed. Fleeting memories brought by the heady fragrance of the honeysuckle lulled Beatty as she picked veggies for a batch of soup, when she was interrupted by a call from Mrs. Parker. The gate creaked open and she said, "Hello, dear, I've been wanting to say how very sorry I am for all your losses. Also, I'm sorry for exposing your secret but it is best that it came out."

"Why, thank you, Mrs. Parker, it has been extraordinarily difficult, I forgive you for reading the letter, forget it, it seems like years ago anyway."

"If you can spare me four of your chook eggs, I've saved enough flour, sugar and butter rations to make you all a cake. I thought the little children could do with a treat."

"Thank you, that would be lovely." Kind acts were few and far between that when they occurred they invariably made Beatty feel teary. The church community had condemned them, all apart from Father O'Malley, and so in her isolation Beatty grabbed at any life lines flung her way. Kabbarli was also a regular visitor, she was highly chuffed that the baby had 'Lena' as part of her name, they really liked her and she tried to be supportive but Beatty felt she wasn't always the most helpful visitor. One time she brought witchetty grubs, which only the boys were game enough to try, "That's a bit of alright," they said, "tastes like chicken." She also brought some bizarre suggestions like why didn't Beatty breast feed the new baby herself. They did try some of her teas and they loved her wattle seed griddle cakes. She didn't usually knock but just stood at the back kitchen door until someone noticed her. She was waiting like a shadow, Beatty got a bit of a shock but called out, "Come in."

She placed a slab of meat with a thud on the table, "Dis roo, good tucker, you make stew for all dem chil'n."

"Thanks, Kabbarli, will you have a cup of tea."

"Yea, I like some lemon grass."

Beatty also had a cup of tea and put a small saucepan of milk on the stove to prepare a bottle for Mary Eliza, and while she waited they sat at the table and chatted. Mother would have been horrified, her entertaining a koori in her kitchen, indeed she was probably turning in her grave.

"I still don't know why you don't feed baby yourself, you should try."

Beatty blushed but lifted up her loose fitting blouse and Kabbarli helped to guide the baby's hungry mouth to her breast. The baby made some frustrated grunting sounds but Kabbarli said that was only because Beatty didn't have a proper milk supply because the baby wasn't born to her. If she persisted it would come in then the baby would only need a bottle when Beatty went to work. Mary fell asleep due to the extra effort required sucking at a real nipple rather than a bottle teat.

"I'll bring you some good herb for milk supply and some milk-wood sap to give you milk."

Beatty finally worked up enough courage to state what was on her mind, "I'm dreadfully worried that I'll die in child birth like Mother, what if I can't cope with all the pain?" she said.

"No, you be right. You young, you strong, you healthy. You tell you self that n be positive. I come back and help you."

"What do you mean, are you leaving?"

"Time go walkabout. Spirits restless. Need to collect more medicine. Is getting colder, I go north. I be back in time for your baby be born."

"But, you've been so helpful . . . so, supportive, whatever am I going to do without you and how will you know when my time is near?"

"You strong, nature mother, earth mother, you be right. Just trust me I know dis thing."

Beatty hugged her as she said goodbye. Tears seemed to well in her eyes constantly these days.

She chopped up the meat into cubes and added it to the soup, letting it boil vigorously to reduce down. She left instructions with Amelia to stir it occasionally. Despite feeling weary she went off to clean at the library, having a perfunctory chat with Mrs. Richardson before she left her to it. She whisked around, looking forward to the hearty stew she knew would be ready when she got home. She sure had a rampant appetite these days. Her baby bump was swelling rapidly too.

The stew smelt delicious as she entered the house. To her surprise, the kitchen had been cleaned spotlessly and the table freshly scrubbed down. A sponge cake sat in the middle, delivered by Mrs. Parker while she was out. Gran sat hunched over the singer sewing machine rocking back and forth with the rhythm of the treadle. She had decided to make Beatty a new expanded waist pinafore out of a double bed sheet, cut economically around the worn thread bare centre. It was a surprise for Beatty. But the biggest and best surprise was that Gran was up and joining in life. Gran also planned to make a little smocked baby's nightie to show she accepted the baby. Tears welled in her eyes for Joyce as she fingered the handmade lace edge on the sheet that she had made for Joyce's trousseau, for her wedding to Charles some eighteen years ago. No wonder it was worn. She battled the feeling of grief, reminding herself that she had a living family who needed her to tend to them.

Dinner was eaten with gusto and everyone one agreed it was the most flavoursome meal Beatty had ever made and they were all so pleased that Gran was up at last. The cake was such a treat that everyone ate far too much which was an unusual occurrence in these days of strict rationing.

The baby was growing well and was really no trouble, but she knew that Beatty was her mother and she cried in the evenings unless Beatty tended to her. Beatty's milk had come in but wasn't enough to supply the growing demand of Mary so she supplemented her appetite with two bottles a day, one was given while Beatty was at work in the afternoon and one in the evening to help her sleep soundly through the night. It was a good opportunity for the other siblings to bond with the baby, sharing the bottle feeding. Now that Gran was up and involved it was a blessed reprieve as it relieved Beatty of any further kitchen duties for the day. The family had grown accustomed to seeing Mary Eliza at Beatty's breast, although Gran was shocked at first, but she accepted it as the most practical healthy way and anyway by the time she noticed, Mary was addicted. After the other children had helped Gran to clean up the dishes, they gathered around the armchair while Beatty resumed reading from 'A Secret Garden'. It had been such a long break it was hard to get back into.

As Beatty laid the sleeping baby in her basket next to her bed, she felt such a gush of love for her. She knew she couldn't love her more if she had given birth to her. She'd fallen head over heels in love with her.

A few days later, just as Beatty had finished bathing Mary and putting fresh clothes on her, there was a knock at the door. Amelia answered and let Mrs. Brownell in.

She was laden with home cooked things, "I'm sorry that I didn't come any earlier. I just wanted you to get accustomed to it and I thought that everyone else would bring food initially. I don't know what to say, words cannot express my sorrow for you." She placed the basket on the table and started unpacking it. "I've made you a steak and kidney pie and my currant slice, Robin said you liked it."

Mary started fussing for a feed so Beatty sat down. Mavis came and gave them both a hug and said, "She's very sweet."

Beatty adjusted her clothes to feed Mary. Initially Mavis was wide eyed with surprise then she said, "Well you are obviously a natural mother, she is looking healthy."

"You can nurse her after she's had a feed if you like."

"Yes, I'd like that very much. Listen to me prattling on, how are you and how are you coping?"

"I'm tired but I love Mary and now that Gran is up more and helping out I'm coping better. I can't bare the thought that I'll never see my parents again. I think about Robin and miss him a lot, have you heard from him?"

Mavis reached into her basket and took out an official looking letter, unfolded it and passed it to Beatty.

Dear Mrs. Robert Brownell,

In response to your letter requesting the whereabouts of your husband, Mr. Robert James Brownell and your son, Master Robin Gerald Brownell, we wish to inform you that the former is recovering from a leg wound and will be shipped home a.s.a.p. As for the later there is still no news as yet.

"What can that mean?" Beatty gave Mavis a piercing look.

"It could mean anything. I'm not worrying, or at least trying not to, yet." Mavis said.

"Well, I guess no news is good news, that's what Dad always used to say," said Beatty trying to be encouraging as much for herself as for Mavis.

There was a tap on the back door and Beatty saw it was Mrs. Parker from next door so she called out for her to come in.

"Just came to get me plate, how was the cake?"

"We all loved it and wolfed it down, you should have seen the children, it was like a birthday party."

"That's good, dear. I've been thinking now that the weather is getting colder and winter is approaching fast and your pregnancy is progressing, that you can use my inside flush toilet instead of battling your old outhouse. Mind my offer is only for you, I don't want all the children trouping through my house."

"My, that is a very kind offer, Mrs. Parker. Thank you. You know how much I hate the spiders in the dunny."

"Ok, that's settled then, I'll put the backdoor key under a terracotta flower pot by the step and you help yourself. I'll be off, bye for now." She grabbed her plate and bustled off.

Beatty was touched by the recent care of a few friends. She reminded herself to focus on the ones that came not the ones who had abandoned them.

"Let me nurse the baby while you do some chores." Beatty gently passed the sleeping infant to Mavis who sat mesmerised by the rhythmic sound of her breathing. It had been too long since she had held a little one, she could get used to this. Beatty went through to the wringer in the laundry to continue with the never ending wash. It was hard on her body, she formed blisters under her calluses and it made her lower back ache, but it had to be done.

Late that night when all the children were sleeping peacefully, Beatty thought about Robin and took out his last letter. His words echoed around in her mind. How could he possibly be lost? She looked for clues but found none. There was no date or place noted on the letter. Her heart felt heavy. What if something had happened to him? What if he was injured? What if he returned disabled? What if he never returned? Perish the thought! She had to be strong and positive. She couldn't afford to entertain demons. She couldn't afford to let negative thoughts prey on her mind. After all they are one and the same, aren't they? Beatty was formulating the thinking that the devil or Satan was simply destructive thought processes. She reached up and pulled the cord to switch off the light.

She found she was so dashed busy during the day that she was distracted but come night and her worries magnified and haunted her and kept her exhausted body from getting the sleep it craved and so desperately needed. She consciously tried to change around her thoughts to create a more positive future but the old ingrained habits had a way of rearing their ugly heads. As the new life within her stirred, filling her with wonder and longing, she wished for Robin to be able to share this miracle with her. She conscientiously listened for the soft rhythmic breath of Mary and the slightly snuffly breath of Evie. She silently prayed to her parents asking them for guidance. Mary stirred and started to whimper, Beatty collected her from the basket, before she disturbed the others, her face and hands were cold so she cradled her close and climbed back into the cosy warmth of her bed and put her to her breast, within minutes they were both asleep.

CHAPTER
SIXTEEN

Queen Bee

The winter cold and damp brought fresh challenges for Beatty and her family. There was a shortage of coal and wood to keep the stove going so they barely kept it alive and she felt that she was constantly nagging the boys to go on the scrounge to collect burnable materials. Gran had taken to her bed as the winter had crept into her joints and taken up residence as inflamed warring soldiers causing her tremendous pain. This meant that Beatty in her ever increasing ungainly condition had to shoulder even more of the responsibility again.

Gran's mood had changed, for the worse and she was taking out her frustration on Beatty, in the form of cutting remarks. Beatty made her up the tea that Kabbarli had brought before she went walkabout, Cunjevoi and Stinging Nettle to relieve her rheumatic pain and both she and Amelia took turns to massage Beatty's cream into her feet and joints, but still Gran was seemingly ruled by the discomfort.

Beatty continued to buoy herself up by conscientiously thinking positive encouraging thoughts and a favourite at the moment was 'the worst of winter is over, the days are getting longer and warmer, spring will be here soon.'

She cleaned down the baby pram and made it up with fresh blankets. She could see what a beautiful crisp winter's day it was and she didn't care how unseemly it appeared to be to go out in public in her ungainly state, she was taking Mary and Evie for a stroll. Mary lulled to sleep easily in the beautiful big wheeled English pram that Mother had bought for Beatty and used for all her babies and Evie was having a lovely time sitting up in her seat enjoying the scenery. They passed some church ladies dressed in their matching twin sets and pearls, she waved and said, "Hello, beautiful day." They ignored her and crossed the street, cruelly snubbing the little trio. 'Nothing,' Beatty muttered and resolved, could spoil her precious day, she wouldn't let it, 'they mean nothing to me.'

Beatty breathed in the fresh air and enjoyed the taste of freedom. It didn't taste like the fresh pure meadow air that she remembered, it was only city air with a hint of wood smoke but it was good compared to inside a stuffy house and shady confined backyard. 'Yes,' she decided she liked the taste of freedom no matter how restrained and she promised herself to do this more often. Gran could feel sorry for herself, and as much as she didn't like to see her suffer, there was only so much she could put up with; she had to get out occasionally for her sanity and to be a better parent.

Beatty knew exactly where she was headed; Harry had brought home a message on his paper route from Mavis that Beatty was to visit as soon as possible. Beatty assumed Mavis had news but for some reason couldn't come around herself. She hesitated before she knocked, butterflies of anticipation fluttering in her tummy. Mavis answered slightly breathless and flustered, hugged Beatty and helped her in with the cumbersome pram.

Mavis whispered, "Bob's home, I'll check to see if he is awake."

Beatty lifted Evie down from her seat and said in a hushed but stern voice, "Don't you dare touch anything, will you?"

Evie shook her head with an innocent earnestness her blonde curls bobbing sweetly. They walked through to the living room where Bob was propped up sideways on the ottoman with tapestry cushions behind him and a crotchet rug over his leg and a depression where the other leg was missing. Beatty didn't know where to look or what to say, so she smiled and went forward to give him a hug. She realised that Bob was the last person to see her Father alive and the emotion welled up and choked her throat, she looked away battling to suppress her tears.

Mavis bustled in and served tea and biscuits acting as if all were totally normal. Bob chatted and showed interest in the children and Beatty's health. She relaxed and started to enjoy herself. Mary woke and Mavis went to collect her as Evie was perched on Beatty's lap. They clucked over her as if she was their natural grandchild. Beatty felt blessed that they clearly loved children. When Bob had to get up to go to the toilet, he swung around on his crutches with practiced agility. Beatty was impressed by what appeared to be his accepting attitude.

Back on the home front the air hung heavy with hostility. Beatty was horrified that an afternoon's outing could cause so much friction. Gran was up and making a performance of putting a simple meal together. Beatty could tell she looked weary but she didn't expect the barrage of insults that she suddenly dumped on her.

"Look at you child, not quite seventeen, gallivanting around the town announcing to all and sundry your shameful condition. Heavily pregnant with an illegitimate . . . bastard baby, as if we haven't got enough mouths to feed. Just as well your parents aren't alive to suffer the shame of it."

Beatty stood there stunned, she knew it was the aching joints complaining but still her blood began to boil and she burst out, "Oh shut up, Gran, that's hardly fair. I work all the time and no-one ever thanks me. I always look after the babies." At this point Evie was fidgeting and Mary started to cry so Beatty had to tend to them and wasn't fully able to vent her own frustration. Gran climbed the stairs moaning and groaning loudly for all to hear.

After the children were fed she finished reading 'The Secret Garden' to them and then blessedly they went to bed cooperatively, Beatty wearily cleaned the kitchen then cleaned out the back room. No-one had been keen to move into the bed that Mother had died in but Beatty knew that sooner or later something had to be done, they simply needed the space. They would all have a shuffle around. Beatty and the babies would share this room, close and practical to the fire and far enough away from the others not to disturb them in the night. She hoped that her Mother's spirit would be benevolent. Gran would move down into Beatty's bed, thus avoiding the stairs and share with Amelia and Harry would move up to her room which used to be the marital bed. She scrubbed and dusted and made the bed up fresh. She supposed that the ghosts of her parents permeated the whole house. It did worry her that this bed with its blood stained mattress might be jinxed, but she checked her thoughts trying not to entertain demons unawares.

On the morning of the fifteenth of August, Beatty woke in her new bed. Her back ached, the mattress was too soft and she lay having a tentative stretch feeling the new life actively moving in her abdomen. She rested her hands on her wobbling abdomen and missed Robin and wished with a deep ache that he was here to share this profound experience with her. She realised it was her seventeenth birthday and her first birthday without her parents. She reminisced about her last birthday, the Secret Garden and stockings birthday; the day Dad and Bob got called up, the day that devastated the rest of her life. Hot tears poured down her cold face. The baby started to cry and Amelia brought her to Beatty and sat on the side of her bed, wishing her a happy day and trying to cheer her up.

They talked about the library job which Amelia had completely taken over now that Beatty was getting too big. Gradually all the family woke and gathered around her wishing her a happy day. Gran was being especially nice to her and even though they usually celebrated together and this year was Gran's big seventieth she placed all the emphasis on Beatty's seventeenth. There were a few little presents and Harry was chuffed that he was able to buy her a little bottle of Tasmanian Lavender Oil with his own hard earned money. Gran had saved up rations and eggs and had organised for Mrs. Parker to bake a cake. Even Mavis dropped around with a gift of a cobalt blue, glass eyebath, probably from one of her collections and a tin of her currant slice. It was a quiet day but everyone was extraordinarily helpful to make it go smoothly. Beatty felt a bit like a queen bee, stretched out, abdomen protruding with all her workers busy buzzing around her. The baby was due any day soon.

The next couple of weeks were to prove a tremendous test to her patience as she waited, feeling like a beached whale and no sign that the baby would be born soon and still no sign of Kabbarli.

"You must have got your dates mixed up," said Gran as she bustled around Beatty as she sat stranded in the kitchen with her feet up.

"No, it'll just be well cooked, I'm waiting for Kabbarli, I reckon."

Beatty tossed and turned that night finding it hard to get comfortable. She started to emit low groans. Amelia came in to check on her and Beatty said for her to go back to bed. Less than an hour later she called for Amelia who went to rouse Gran and also Harry.

Gran was immediately awake and fully efficient, directing Harry to stoke up the fire then go fetch the doctor. Instead Harry went via Kabbarli's humpy and called out to her. She had arrived home the night before and planned to visit early in the morning anyway. They grabbed her supplies and hastened back. The whole household was awake when they arrived home and warmer than it had been all winter. Beatty was moving about and rocking when a strong contraction gripped her.

Gran muttered, "Hail Mary, full of grace . . . ."

"Oh, for heaven's sake Gran, shut up." Beatty retorted.

Kabbarli said, "You do good girl, you strong, it natural thing to do. You hold you baby soon." As she half hugged her and rubbed her lower back.

"What if the pains get stronger? I couldn't stand anymore," Beatty asked in a pleading voice.

"Not long now girl, stay positive."

Gran and Kabbarli guided her to the room behind the grey blanket curtain, just in time for Beatty to grab the cast iron bed end and give a long low groan. Kabbarli lifted up her white cotton nightie and tied it above her abdomen. Gran wiped some bloody membrane away from Beatty's thighs with an old towel. "Push now, just pant . . . now big push . . . you can do it," directed Kabbarli.

Between Beatty's legs, Kabbarli was knelt down to guide the baby out. With a tremendous contraction and moan, the new life thrust into the competent healing hands. A moment later the gusty cry of a newborn baby filled the air. Gran had a heated towel ready to wrap it up in. Beatty felt light headed. They helped her onto the bed and handed her baby to her. Tears of joy and relief tinged with sadness flowed down her face. She lifted the corner of the towel and checked out her baby. Yes, ten fingers, ten toes, healthy lungs, an exquisitely perfect baby girl. She had sort of hoped for a boy for Robin but secretly she was pleased to have a girl, she had lots of experience with baby girls. Beatty passed the placenta easily and the women worked as a fantastic team cleaning up.

Once again Kabbarli sent the boys to collect wattle twigs to make a small fire to smoke the infant. But this time Gran was also on board to use more English traditions and after smoking, the baby was bathed and dressed in a soft viyella nightie. Gran sent Harry to fetch the priest to bless the baby with holy water. Beatty was cleaned up and positioned up in bed for all the family to visit her and the new addition. Evie wasn't sure about this new 'doll' and she lashed out at the baby and Beatty had to elbow her to collect the blow. They would have to watch this one. Harry had to race off to do his deliveries and Amelia had to go to work at the library.

Beatty dozed with her daughter at her breast and when she woke she realised that the date was the first of September, the first day of spring. What an auspicious birth-date! This augured well for new beginnings.

Beatty could hear a heated argument in the kitchen, and the grey curtain fluttered and Gran peeked her head around, "Oh, good you're awake, sorry if we woke you, but we can't agree on something."

Kabbarli also appeared around the curtain. "She," Gran said indicating Kabbarli "wants to cook up the placenta for your breakfast, and I want you to have porridge."

"Is good, make you strong," explained Kabbarli.

No matter how bored Beatty was with porridge she didn't think she could stomach her own placenta fried up for breakfast. "I really want to have the placenta planted under the Daphne bush by the back door, give it back to the earth. Would you mind very much?" She asked.

"Is good, not waste, it a bit gritty anyway, too overdue. I go now, see you tomorrow."

Gran was relieved to be in charge again.

Harry had delivered the exciting news with the morning newspapers and later that morning Bob and Mavis visited with gifts and fresh baked goodies to see their first grandchild. They looked down at the peacefully sleeping child and saw their own son nestled in her features. Tears welled in their eyes.

"What have you decided to call her?" asked Mavis.

"I like 'Jenny', do you?" Beatty said.

"Jenny, yes, that is fresh and childlike, hello, and welcome, little Jenny," she smiled down at the baby.

Jenny fed well and grew well, she was an easy baby and everyone adored her. At times Evie and Mary felt left out and would deliberately pinch the baby but they all tried to give them attention too. Beatty tandem fed both Mary and Jenny partly because she had ample milk but also because so couldn't bear to cut Mary off suddenly. She hoped it would help the babies bond as well. There were so many demands to Beatty's time, what with two little breast fed babies, Evie and a household to run, she was fulfilled as a new mother but still she felt like something was missing. Something apart from Robin!

As Beatty was dozing with both babies feeding in bed, Gran came in to check on her. "Bea, I'm sorry I've been crabby lately, me arthritic pain got me down. I want you to know I think you are doing a great job. I should be able to help out more now the weather is getting warmer." She shook out the silk sari quilt that Bob had sent back from war on behalf of Father as a farewell gift for Mother, and spread it over Beatty and the babies. "I'm sure your parents would have wanted you to have this." Beatty choked up.

Many months later and the nagging thought that something was missing continued, Beatty decided she would have do something with her mind and her life so she loaded the three small girls into the front of the truck and drove them to the Brownell's residence for a visit.

They treated Evie, Mary and Jenny like grandchildren, doting on them all and spoiling them equally. As each adult sat with a child balanced on their knee, Beatty suddenly asked, "Bob, I want to get the bee business up and running again, will you help me?"

"Blimey Lass, I don't see how much help I could be, in my state." He said indicating his missing leg.

"You wouldn't have to do anything, just give me advice on how to get it started again."

"Well, I suppose, but it is a huge undertaking, the boxes are diseased. Don't you already have enough on your plate?" Bob asked.

"I know but I feel like I need something more . . . satisfying in my life, and I always loved the bees. If I get it started Robin can take over when he returns from war, you could do the paperwork, Harry can help out and it would be a good business for the twins to grow into. After all the factory is just sitting there."

"Well, it could be worth a go, but only if you can manage. I've got a few books you can read up."

When Beatty arrived home feeling inspired and with renewed energy she was pleased to see Amelia was massaging Gran's feet. "Mrs. Richardson wants to know when you can take over the job at the library." Amelia said.

In her new found enthusiasm she replied, "Anytime, tomorrow if you like."

CHAPTER
SEVENTEEN

Backyard Bees

Spring brought with it the promise of new hope. As the days grew warmer and longer, Beatty felt her strength and 'Jolie de vivre' return. Sure she had to be extremely well organised and stick to a disciplined routine in order to juggle feeding the babies, her twice daily job at the library and domestic chores. Gran and Amelia had almost entirely taken over the kitchen and laundry duties, all apart from using the mangle which was too heavy for them and Beatty was still in charge of making and baking bread.

The pride she had always felt in her job at the library returned and it also gave her the solitude she needed for her peace. During a short break in the late afternoon cleaning session she would sit on the bench at the freshly polished table and look at and study any books she could find on beekeeping. There were lots of English books, some American but very few Australian which meant that the specifics for seasonal care were all topsy-turvy . . . this lead her to thinking that perhaps there was a demand for an Australian Beekeeping Guide. She realised that cleaning and salvaging the frames would be an enormous task, she would have to get the whole family on board. She arranged for Harry to come straight home after his deliveries, as she would, too, from her morning time at the library, she would feed the babies and leave them in Gran and Amelia's care. She and Harry would drive by the Brownell's to pick up Bob then they would go to the factory to assess the degree of damage.

A cold eerie chill greeted them as they opened the factory warehouse side door. The stench of rodents filled their nostrils. It was like stepping back in time. It was as if this building had been abandoned just as the bees had deserted the diseased hives when they realised that the mummified liquid larvae could not be saved. So too had Robin abandoned the boxes in his overwhelming despair, the hive tool stuck out ominously from one of the grooves, seemingly suspended in time and space. Bob shook his head, "It's bad, Beatty." He crutched his way through the cluttered storeroom and looked into the boxes. "Poor lad, he must have felt just dreadful to leave it in such a mess." Beatty was relieved that she had company for this task.

"But, is any of it salvageable?" She couldn't bare the thought of all her hopes and dreams being dashed, "please say it is."

"Well, it'll take a lot of work but I think it might be. We'll have to scrape all the old honey comb off, burn it and heat sterilize the remaining frames and boxes. Also, we'll have to be extremely careful to remove all traces so as not to contaminate the new hives."

Firstly, they sorted out cardboard boxes, removed cobwebs and swept up. The place had been overrun with rats and mice so there was a lot of cleaning to do. They burnt some watermarked newspapers and rat gnawed cardboard in the drum heater. As it chuffed away it took the chill off the air and gave a more friendly, welcoming atmosphere. Bob sat by the fire and scraped the dark distorted honeycomb off the frames while Beatty and Harry did the more active work. They found a large tin full of honey, from two seasons ago, plenty of boxes of honeycomb sheet which hadn't been totally destroyed by rats and also a large block of propolis, the dark sealing substance that the bees use as an antiseptic in the hive and now it was gaining recognition for human application. The supply of labels and jars could be sorted and cleaned up. She de-cantered some honey into jars, two for home and one each as for gifts for Mavis, Kabbarli and Mrs. Parker.

By the afternoon, the whole warehouse was looking clearer and a jolly good start had been made. The sun streamed in the top windows and dust played and danced in swirls on the convection current. When they called it quits for the day, Beatty dropped Bob back home, changed and cleaned herself up, fed the babies and drove to the library for the late afternoon clean. After she had cleaned the toilet and porcelain hand basin, she took a brief break and she looked up obtaining new hives and wrote to the only local address, but still some distance away on Wattle Hill via Caveat off Goulburn Valley Highway, in the back of a book, explaining her situation and asking after availability. That night she fell into bed extremely tired but with such a deep sense of satisfaction, she knew she had done the right thing. She felt sure Father was feeling proud of her and smiling down on her.

A week later she received a letter from the beekeeper, Arthur Goldman saying that if she was quick in preparing herself she could have three of his swarms when they flew, near the spring equinox. 'But that is only days away.' When she realised that, she panicked and went back to the factory after the babies were fed and in bed for the night. She used a blow torch to sterilize the frames and boxes, it was tricky work, having just enough heat to do the job but not to set them on fire, nearby she had a basin of water to plunge the smouldering wood into, should it catch alight. She promised herself that if and when the business was successful again she would have new freshly painted, white boxes. She patched up some the remaining rat-gnawed honeycomb and attached it to the frames, stacking and layering the boxes in the correct order. It was very cold and late by the time she went home and she lay in bed shivering until she fell asleep.

After work in the morning she asked Mrs. Parker if she could use her telephone to ring the number in the letter. She arranged for the beekeeper to call Mrs. Parker and leave a message for Beatty when the swarming happened.

Harry helped Beatty to load the three complete units onto the truck tray and tied them on firmly in order to be prepared for whenever the call came through.

Days passed and Beatty despaired of ever hearing. In her excitement it was hard to wait patiently. All the rush to get ready to just end up with time to spare waiting. Still there was plenty to get on with.

The middle of the day routine was established and Beatty, Harry and Bob worked amicably and jovially together. "I swear you saved me pride n me marriage by dragging me back here," said Bob one lunch break. "Sure," Beatty replied, "n I saved me own sanity, I was going crazy in that little house with all those hungry mouths to feed. A least this way we have the start of a better future to look forward to."

Early next morning as Beatty stealthily let herself in Mrs. Parker's back door for her morning ablutions, she gasped in shock as she very nearly walked into a returned soldier in full khaki uniform. For a moment she thought it was Robin and she did a double take, "I'm sorry, I just have an understanding with Mrs. Parker, I'll go, so sorry." She turned to flee when Mrs. Parker arrived in her night attire and said, "Ah, Beatty, you remember my son Eddie, don't you? He's home early, he was injured . . . he lost his arm." Beatty saw where his left sleeve was pinned back, she was embarrassed and lost for words,

"I'm sorry, I'll go." She turned swiftly on her heel and fled to the old familiarity of the wooden dunny seat, 'That'll be the last time I go there.' She said as she cradled her flushed face in her hands.

After cleaning at the library she decided she wouldn't go to the warehouse, she had a hunch that surely it would be today, she had to be near Mrs. Parker's phone for the swarm call so she helped Gran with a spring clean while Amelia looked after the babies. She tied her hair up in a scarf to keep the dust out while she beat the living daylights out of the mats draped over the line. She scrubbed out the dunny and removed all the spider's webs. She scrubbed the kitchen floor and was just about to toss the contents of the bucket out the back door when she saw someone standing there and she stopped herself mid swing. It was Mrs. Parker's son, still dressed in his uniform. "Mum, said for me to deliver a message to you, a telephone call came for you, the bees are swarming."

"Oh, blast," she replied, "I don't even know where Harry is."

"I could come and help you if you like."

"I doubt it, you wouldn't be much help in your condition," she replied tactlessly. She saw a dark look cross his face, she back tracked, "I'm so sorry, that was thoughtless."

"Well, you would be surprised." He saluted, turned on his heel and left.

Beatty grabbed her bag of beekeeping clothes, pulled off her hair covering, kissed the babies and headed off. She wasn't really sure where this beekeeper lived even, but hopefully not too far, somewhere near the Goulburn Valley River, he'd drawn a mud map of sorts, and the order of the little towns to pass through, which he had included in his note. She cranked over the truck, swore and climbed in. As she drove she thought of her shock to see Mrs. Parker's handsome son and her unkind response to his injury. She must have hurt his pride, she felt ashamed and sorry. She emerged from the suburban sprawl of Melbourne and travelled along a pitted dirt track, the road seemed endless, it was much farther than she had thought. She suspected that she had gotten lost while she had allowed her thoughts to distractedly meander. She stopped at a farmhouse to ask directions. She had to back track a little, she had missed the turn off. Finally she saw the sign, 'Goulburn Honey Farm.' She turned in and apologised to the farmer that it took her so long.

"Arthur Goldman," he thrust out his hand to shake hers, "Pleased to meet you." His eyes sparkled in his weather beaten but pleasant smiling face, his voice was warm and jovial and Beatty immediately felt as ease with him. He was already dressed in his white beekeeping overalls. She shook his hand, "Beatrice Fielding, I appreciate all your help. I'll just put my overalls on." He had caught the swarms in cardboard boxes and showed Beatty how to shake them into their new homes, making sure to identify that the queen bee was installed in each box. While the bees settled in to their new boxes he invited Beatty in for a cup of tea. His wife, Elsie was a plump, good natured domestic queen and she bustled about the kingdom of her kitchen and brought a tray of tea things and bikkies out onto the veranda where they sat, then she retreated back inside, her floral dress swishing as she walked leaving them to share in their fascination of bee stories. They shared an affinity of the bees and talked of the harmonious hierarchy in the colonies. Beatty had only ever listened to her Father talk like this before, now she was older, had studied and observed, she felt the wonder too. He advised Beatty to keep the new bees in her backyard to keep an eye on them; he thought given their history that it was too far to go to Greendale to check on just three hives. The setting sun cast a lovely peachy glow along the Goulburn Valley; she loved the area and wished for a quiet country life and space around her.

"I feel so relaxed here; I would love to live here."

"Yes, Else and I love it, too. Although it is getting to be too much work now we are older. We weren't blessed with any children so it is just the two of us."

"How much land do you have?" Beatty asked.

"About five hundred acres, some is bush, there's the stone fruit orchard and the bees and their pastures, so it's a lot of work for an old codger, like me."

"You're not old," Beatty said. He helped her tape up the boxes and tie them down securely then he cranked over the truck for her and she was off, kangaroo hopping down the drive, still conscious of people watching her driving.

As she drove home she thought about his placement advice, Gran would probably think it was unseemly but it was the most practical method, the more she thought of it the happier she felt about it. She leant forward and peered through the windscreen, watching and swerving for native animals on the road. This was her first night drive and she saw a slow meandering possum whose eyes glowed red in the truck head lights and had a rush of adrenaline as a wallaby bounded out suddenly across her path making her skid a bit on the gravel as she applied the brakes too much. Her concentration was all but spent from straining to see by the dim headlights. She was relieved when she arrived in the familiar suburb.

She was weary as she drove home but knew that she had to unload tonight so that the bees didn't get confused. She left the truck running as she called for Harry to give her a hand, the household was in pandemonium with both little babies crying for her. "They'll just have to wait, Gran, I won't be too long."

She drove around the back down the narrow sanitary lane. The truck lights were rather dim and when it came time to reverse to get to the back gate Beatty scraped along the paling fence at the back of Mrs. Parker's place. Eddy came out to see what all the commotion was about, "How about I back up for you as you direct me?" He called out.

By now Beatty was so flustered and frustrated that she accepted. He smoothly maneouvered the truck into place, jumped out, climbed onto the tray and helped to move the boxes with his strong arm and powerful other shoulder. The three of them were able to position the boxes in no time at the back of the side fence. He then offered to un-tape them and finish up while Beatty went in to feed the howling babies. He and Harry closed up the gate then drove around the block and parked in the front of the house in the usual position. Beatty was weary and longed for a freshen up but tended to the unsettled babies first. Relieved they slept easily; Beatty fell into bed without any dinner.

Months passed and a positive routine was established. Beatty enjoyed being at the library, especially when Mrs. Richardson took time off and she was able to fill the role of librarian. The babies were growing well and had gotten accustomed to the shared care but still knew that Beatty was their mother. The bees were buzzing merrily, happily collecting the summer nectar and pollen from the suburban blossoms. Gran had accepted the sense in having them close at hand. They really took care of themselves and having only three hives was very little work. The warehouse was in good condition and all the other hives were ready for collecting swarms next spring, or earlier if she could source a queen breeder. Mostly Beatty was contented, but she hadn't heard from Robin lately.

Eddie popped in from time to time to assist, he was very skilful with repairs and even though he only had the one arm he was remarkably capable. One beautiful settled autumn day he said to Beatty, "How about we go for a picnic by the river on Sunday?"

"No, I don't think so," she replied.

"Go on with you," said Gran from the next room, "It'll do you lots of good to take a break from all the hard work you do. Go and get some sunshine."

"No, I have to do some gardening."

"I'll help you do that on Saturday afternoon, then." Eddie offered.

"Ok, I suppose so, if Gran says so," she replied.

Sunday dawned and Beatty reluctantly prepared things for the picnic. She dressed the girls up and packed their coats in case it turned cold. She packed the picnic basket with whatever leftovers she could find, then she put Jenny in the pram, Mary sat in the over seat and Evie was tied on to the handle with a white leather harness, so she couldn't do a runner. She maneuvered her load along the passage and out the front door, then went back to collect the basket and an old tartan rug. When Eddie answered her knock, he raised his eyebrows in surprise at all the entourage, but he good naturedly said, "Right you are, beautiful day, ain't it?" and grabbed the basket. Beatty pushed the unwieldy load along the street. She headed towards the river, where Kabbarli camped.

Eddie tried to make conversation, but to no avail, until he asked about the bees, then Beatty answered animatedly. They found a grassy knoll and spread out the rug and she sat the children on it. Then she went to the edge of the clearing to the bush where Kabbarli lived and called her over. Beatty was thinking that she could shock Eddie. When Kabbarli arrived smelling strongly of campfire, Eddie stood up and walked towards her and gave her a hug.

"My, lad you've grown up," she said. Beatty looked shocked at the easy acquaintance so by way of explanation Eddie said, "I grew up on her lotions and potions, since I was wee high," and he indicated with his hand, measuring at his knees.

They shared their lunch and joked together. The little children had roses in their cheeks and Beatty relaxed and enjoyed herself.

As they walked back, Eddie said, "I know you feel awkward about my missing arm and arm stump but I want you to know I've applied for an artificial arm."

"No, it's alright," Beatty protested, "it doesn't bother me, truly."

It had been a bad day for Mrs. Morton, she'd put her book down earlier and couldn't settle. She opened and closed the cupboard doors and the drawers, looking for something but couldn't quite remember what.

Jennifer tapped on the door and came in.

"Oh, there you are," Mrs. Morton said, "What have you done with all my precious stuff? Where is it all?"

Jennifer sighed, "Come now, Mum, you know anything you ever had of any value was either burnt, buried, backed into or bummed off. I haven't got it squirreled away anywhere, I promise," she pulled the bedspread straighter, "I have, however, brought you the usual installment of Lindt chocolate."

Mrs. Morton's face softened and she smiled, she reached out for the blue packet, rubbing her hands together, "Oh, goody, my fav," and in a fleeting moment of clarity she said, "thank you, my dear, you really are good to me, despite my crankiness."

Jennifer kissed her forehead and left. Mrs. Morton unwrapped the foil and popped a square of chocolate in her mouth. She pottered around her room, straightening up her things. Her hands shook as she squirreled away chocolate pieces in obscure place. She put a piece in each zippered section of her toiletry bag, one inside her jewellery box, in her bedside drawer . . . When she came across an old previously hidden one under an ornament, she popped it in her mouth and detected orange flavour, a bit dusty and a bit stale. She worked methodically, hiding them away, wondering if anyone would be able to crack her secret code on how to find them again.

She walked down the corridor and stood at the barred double doors, she tried to open them but they wouldn't budge. She stood looking at the security box, wondering if she would be able to crack that code. She tried a few combinations, but when they didn't work she triggered the alarm and an orderly rushed towards her and said, "C'mon, Mrs. Morton, I'll take you down to the day room and you can talk to your friends and watch some telly."

"No, I don't feel like it." She said, but, despite her protests she was helped into a padded vinyl armchair. She didn't like the day room much, it smelt stuffy and like babies' nappies.

The old man, Edward, who had cornered her many times before and she suspected was very keen on her, started chatting to her as if he knew all about her. She wasn't interested so she wandered back to her room and sank into her armchair and continued reading, skipping ahead to the next chapter.

CHAPTER
EIGHTEEN

Lavish Feast

Life continued and so did the sodding war. Beatty assumed the role of her parents who she deeply missed but as it was now the two year anniversary since their deaths she felt that she had been forced to adjust, prematurely out of increased responsibility. Sure she still pined for them, especially Father. It was hard for Mary Elisa because they couldn't celebrate her birthday without it being tinged with sadness. But, life was busy and they all had to be resolute. As Amelia was turning sixteen soon and going through a very difficult time, Beatty was baffled and didn't really know what to do with her, she remembered it was a confusing time and chastised herself for not being a good role model, but she couldn't help thinking that life would be so much easier if Mother were here. She was sure that Father would be impressed by the beekeeping, she still kept three boxes in the backyard so that the whole family could learn and they also served as her control for the sixty hives she also had at Greendale. These were her 'suburban bees' who gave her an idea of when she had to go out to check on the health and condition of the 'bush bees.'

She couldn't help thinking that Father would be mighty proud of her amazing effort. As yet it wasn't really profitable as she'd had expenses to get re-established but it wouldn't be long. So many people had gotten involved, Bob, of course, who had always had an affinity with bees, Harry who was proving to be a good worker, and quite a budding apiarist, when he was there, even Eddie showed a strong interest and was always willing to lend a hand. Beatty viewed him as a big brother and constantly dropped reminders about her betrothal to Robin and how she couldn't wait for the end of the war and his return.

She and Gran had established an evening routine that when the children were all in bed they sat in the sitting room listening to the radio, sometimes Eddie joined them for supper. Gran usually knitted and Beatty sat with her Beekeeping Journal, filling in the daily entry. She had decided that when she had kept it for three years following the Australian seasons, and honouring Father's precious rule of three, she would sent it in to the Beekeeper's Guild to see if they wanted to publish it. The radio was aural wallpaper, fading in and out of her consciousness with her degree of concentration. They liked to tune in to Australian Broadcasting Commission for the nine o'clock evening news and they usually listened to Mr. Priestly with his postscripts to the evening news. The radio kept them informed on the latest updates making them feel more connected and less isolated. They also enjoyed it when the content was light and frivolous to distract them from their otherwise seriously heavy lives.

One Sunday afternoon, Beatty sat with a cup of tea and listened to Mr. Middleton dispensing advice on gardening. She craned forward to listen past the crackling reception of the radio when Eddie called out and came in. "Hello, Beatty, beautiful day, thought you might like to go for a stroll, just the two of us. Would you?"

"Oh, not now, Eddie, I'm listening to what veggies I have to plant for winter."

"You know, you really ought to let me retune that beast of yours, it's actually right up my line of work."

"Ok," she replied exasperated by the strain, "after I listen to my gardening show, if you do a good job, then I'll go for a walk with you."

"Right you are, it's a deal." Eddie walked through to find the twins on the pavement playing with their marbles. All the family liked Eddie and he often joined in with the children's games, it was also therapeutic for him to play and accept his life change after the horrors he had witnesses. He loved the busy alive family life here in contrast to his mother's home where it was so quiet and she was often pensive wondering after his brother and other relatives back in England.

After her program, Eddie tweaked the radio and repositioned the aerial wire and the new reception was crystal clear in comparison.

Gran urged her to go for a walk with Eddie so she wrapped her soft shawl around her shoulders and they went outside. The shadows were growing longer and there was a crisp autumn chill in the air. Eddie put his arm around Beatty and she enjoyed the warmth of his body. Their conversation was stilted and awkward as it always was when they were on their own away from the hub-bub of the family. Beatty thought back to her friendship with Robin, sure it was a bit awkward at first but it wasn't long before they had developed an easy affection. She had seen Eddie regularly for a couple of years yet she couldn't imagine life without Robin. She made sure he knew she was waiting for him. She hadn't heard anything from him for two years yet she had to hope for the best and assume any mail had gone missing.

Beatty was trying to calculate the summer honey harvest and balance the books one evening as the 'Radio Doctor' dispensed advice on health and fitness. She twirled the end of her pencil in her mouth, 'That's funny,' she muttered as furrows knitted on her brow.

"What is?" asked Gran.

"Wow! That is odd!" Beatty exclaimed and turned the lined book around to show her Gran. "Look here, this shows that each of the suburban hives produced three times the equivalent of the quantity to each of the hives to the bush bees."

"So it does, that is interesting. Sure that you haven't made a mistake? You sure made that sound confusing to me." She asked knowing that mathematics was never Beatty's strong point.

"No, I've reworked it lots. I wonder why? Maybe the plants in the garden . . . or maybe it's because they don't have to travel as far, I wonder. I'll go see Arthur on Sunday afternoon at Goulburn Bee Farm, he's been like a mentor to me, he'll know."

One afternoon when Beatty arrived at the library she was amazed at how busy it was. Mrs. Richardson asked her to help serve a customer. A tall handsome stranger was waiting, "May I help you?" Beatty asked.

"Yes, I'm looking for business books; can you lead me in the right direction?" Beatty felt the old familiar flutter of excitement inside. She flushed and said, "Follow me." She was sure that her hips sashayed more than usual and she was also sure she could feel a burning heat on her derriere, if she looked around she was sure she would catch his eyes on her bottom.

"Any business in particular?" she asked.

"Yes, as a matter of fact, I'm an accountant."

"Oh, are you?"

"Well, almost. By the way, my name is Darren. Perhaps I could take you out to afternoon tea sometime?"

"Thank you, but no. Actually, I'm waiting for my fiancé to return from war." Beatty replied. "I could however, do with some help with accounting." Not wanting to completely sever the excitement she felt with this charming man.

"Sure, and I won't charge you as much if you let me take you to dinner, Saturday? Deal?" Well, Beatty couldn't see the good reckoning in that but she was charmed she admitted and so she agreed.

Saturday arrived none too fast. She reminded herself it was a business deal and that she wasn't being disloyal to Robin, it was just dinner. This handsome stranger might be able to charm her to dinner but it wasn't like she could be charmed away from her beloved, Robin.

In the afternoon, the whole family was in the back garden working and playing at assorted things, when suddenly Evie gave a blood curdling scream. Beatty rushed over and bobbed down, throwing her arms around Evie, "What's the matter, sweetheart, where are you hurt?"

Evie's beautiful big blue eyes were filled with tears and she shoved out her hand. A bee had stung her. It was angry, red and swelling. Beatty tweezed out the sting with her fingernails.

In between sobs, Evie said, "You said bees won't hurt you, they are your friends." It was a statement but her eyes were full of questions.

"Right, that's it! The bees will have to go from the backyard. It simply isn't big enough," said Gran.

"No, Gran, we can't. It's the first time anyone has been stung in the garden and I'm on the verge of a major discovery. These bees are amazing, they are our best producers."

"Well, I won't have it. It's not like the children can be banned from the backyard, is it?"

"Gran, please, we'll talk about it later." Beatty guided Evie in to apply some of her cream and within minutes the sting and itch had gone.

Beatty started to get ready for her dinner business date. She washed her hair and smoothed on her lavender cream. Gran had altered one of Mother's dresses from her younger years as Beatty's Sunday best was looking worn.

Harry answered the door and called, "Your Beau is here." Beatty blushed and biffed him on the arm as she went past.

It was the first time that Beatty had ever gone out to dinner and she felt it was a very elegant affair. She asked him, "Do you have a girlfriend?"

"Sort of, sort of not," he replied, "it's not serious, she'd like it to be, but she isn't really my type, if you know what I mean."

"Sure, I do. Sounds like Eddie, our neighbour. He is very sweet but he lost an arm in the war. I like him as a friend, same thing." She felt they were bonding. Beatty mentioned her observations with the honey harvest, as well as Evie's bee sting.

"Actually, I've been going over your figures over the last couple of evenings and I must say I'm most impressed. When all the payments come in for the summer harvest, you'll be very well off. You ought to think about using some of your profit as a deposit to buy land. I could help you get a bank loan, now I'm your accountant."

Beatty was taken aback, "I've always wanted to do that," she said. "But . . . don't you think it is too early?"

"Not at all, it is a very sound business." He said as he refilled her glass with red wine. Beatty went on to tell him about the devastating brood disease which ruined the whole colony; she was starting to feel light-headed. "Don't worry, I'll take out business insurance to cover you."

He had escorted her as a gentleman all evening, opening the door, pulling out her seat, being an attentive listener, even giving her his jacket against the cold night air. He put his arm around her and guided her along. She gave the odd stumble.

"I think I might be drunk," she said unnecessarily, knowing full well it was the contributing factor to her giddiness.

At the next corner, the gentleman departed as Darren spun her into him and started groping her breasts and bottom and kissing her forcefully on the lips. She tried pushing him away and said, "I told you I am betrothed."

"Come on, pretty lady, you know you want me . . . it's not like you've never done it before."

"No, unhand me this instant, Sir!"

Her head instantly cleared and she started walking briskly along the street.

"I'm sorry, Beatty; I don't know what overcame me back there. Please forgive me. Don't be cross. It won't happen again. I promise." They walked home in stilted silence.

The next day a beautiful bunch of deep pink, long stemmed roses were delivered with a note of apology. Beatty accepted them, both.

Winter proved long and hard, Gran was bed ridden a lot of the time and when she was up she complained bitterly. Beatty's work load increased again. She was trying to be positive, using affirmations consciously and she found it easy enough when she was with Bob and Mavis but often became aware of the negative thought processes when she was at home and so much fell to her. At times she felt she was the only one trying to make positive changes in her family and life. When the winter solstice past she reminded herself that the days would get longer and warmer, every night when she retired with weary despondency she told herself that everything will be brighter in the morning light.

On the morning of the fifteenth of August, 1945, Beatty woke feeling full of hope and excitement, today she turned nineteen. She lay in bed enjoying the cosy warmth. She'd heard Harry steal out to do his rounds, he'd surprised and impressed her with his commitment to his job, and he'd grown taller and stronger in character as well as form. The rest of the house hold was stirring and Beatty supposed she had better get up and light the stove to make breakfast, but it felt so good in bed and after all she rarely stayed in bed and it was her birthday. Gradually little toasty warm bodies climbed into bed with her. Amelia came, sat on the edge of her bed and wished her a happy birthday, and that set off a chorus of breathy wishes and wet kisses from her chubby pink cheeked nightie clad little girls.

She heard Gran get up and start the fire. Suddenly, Harry burst in and shouted, "Have you heard the news? The war is over!" They all hurriedly got dressed in their woollens and were jumping up and down with excitement. Beatty ran to the windows and tore off the blackout. The little terrace house seemingly flooded with light. They heard a commotion on the streets and went to join in the merry throng, the whole suburb of people was spilling out of their houses in various states of dress and were heading down the street to the corner store where a mass of people were congregating with a festive atmosphere. Eddie found Beatty in the crowd, Jenny on her hip and Mary by her side and he hugged her, kissed her and whispered, "Isn't this the best birthday present ever?"

Harry said to Mr. Brown, "Well, I guess I won't have to deliver the papers now that everyone is here to collect them themselves."

"No, n bonus, lad, I'll still pay thee." He replied.

When the excitement died down, Eddie walked home with them and said, "Let's all go to the beach for a day trip, to celebrate your birthday and the end of the war. My treat, I'll pay for the bus fares."

"Yes, let's Bea," all the children piped in.

Back at home, Beatty organised some gear and food, Gran said, "I'll stay at home, I'm too old to go on a bus to the beach, no 'almost spring' birthday trip for me anymore. Anyway, I'd like to have the house to myself; it's been years since it has been quiet here. You all go and have a great time. I'll get the fire hot so there is water for bathing later. I'll even make a lavish feast."

"Thanks, Gran that would be lovely." Beatty said.

When all nine of them were ready to go they walked down the street. Eddie had a back-pack on his back with towels and some home baked goodies. The bus driver let them on for free spontaneously feeling the elation of the day. The children were so excited on the bus and they chatted merrily and joined in with travelling songs. Beatty held Jenny on her lap, she pulled back her soft blonde curly hair and noticed how long her neck was getting, how much she had grown up and how ram-rod straight she held her back. She felt an overwhelming love for her, she kissed her on the neck and smelt her sweet freshness and gave her a squeeze. This spring her baby, her little Jenny wren, would be turning two, where had her tender babyhood gone? Eddie looked over their heads at Beatty and they shared a moment of sheer joy.

The three youngest children had never been to the beach, and the twins could barely remember it. They were in awe of the vastness and the continuous motion of the waves. Beatty sat on a towel on the beach making sandcastles with the girls while the boys braved the cold sea and went in for a dip with Eddie; they laughed and jumped the waves but didn't stay in long. When he walked back up the beach in his snug fitting bathing togs and bare chest, his arm stump looking reddened from the cold water, Beatty flushed and didn't know where to look.

The boys dried themselves off and went up to a multi-coloured boat shed to get dressed. They came back carrying ice-creams in waffle cones. This was also a first for most of the children and became the highlight of the day for most of them.

The bus trip home was subdued, Jenny slept on Beatty's lap, Mary and Evie were leant into Eddie, Gregory and Rupert dozed and all the other were absorbed in their own thoughts and the exhilarating afterglow that only a day at the beach can bring. They walked wearily from the bus stop looking forward to a bath, soup and bed. Beatty thought that this had been the very best birthday she could remember since her parents' deaths.

The smell of cake greeted them and she knew that Gran had been busy while they were out. The house was completely silent, "Yoo-hoo, Gran, are you awake?"

"Through here in the kitchen, dear."

The tired and bedraggled but contented family spilled into the kitchen. Instantly Beatty sensed that something was horribly wrong. Mrs. Brownell sat at the kitchen table with Gran, who said quietly, "Sit down Beatty, I'll make you a cup of tea, Mrs. Brownell has some news. Amelia, take the children into the sitting room for a while." Jenny clung to Beatty so she stayed sitting on her lap.

"I have bad news Beatty," Mavis said, the grief hung heavy in her voice and eyes. The elation of the day plummeted, there was no lavish feast awaiting except the lavish feast of emotion.

CHAPTER
NINETEEN

Soul Sadness

Tears welled in Mavis' eyes as she passed an official looking letter across the table to Beatty. She read:

> Dear Mrs. Brownell,
>
> In response to your enquiry about your son, Master Robin Gerald Brownell, we can only assume he was captured and perished in a Jap P.O.W. camp. We have no record or sightings of him for over twelve months. We have made enquiries on your behalf and unfortunately this poor news is the best we can do. We are very sorry for your loss.
>
> On Behalf of the Royal Australian Army.

The room started to spin and Beatty choked up, she buried her face in Jenny's back, then abruptly handed Jenny over to Gran and she tore off outside as uncontrollable sobs welled up.

She crouched on the low stone wall next to the dunny. She was floored. She'd tried to be totally positive and imagine Robin home soon; she hadn't entertained the demons of death and no return. How could this be happening? He had to be coming home soon. She'd waited for him for almost three years. She curled up and sobbed into her arms. Time stood still. The cool August air crept into her bones, yet she didn't notice. She felt like there was an unfathomable sadness deep in her core at her very soul. When she felt that there wasn't another tear she could cry, she became aware of nature in motion all around her. The last of the bees returning to their hives for the night, streaks of pastel sunset colours spreading across the sky, birds giving a final exuberant chorus before retiring to their nests for the night, the breeze on her face and the smell of the garden waking up for spring.

Her insides felt hollow, like she would never know the sweet fullness of life again. She reached forward and through her blurry vision she plucked a yellow calendula flower. She picked off the petals one by one and said, 'Mother Nature, comfort me in my hour of need, bring me peace, love, harmony and understanding.' She continued to repeat this liturgy to comfort herself until she felt quite light headed and positive. Her vision cleared, it was getting dark and she knew she had to hold it together for the children's sakes. She stood and stretched up, straightening and putting her shoulders back. She gulped to clear the huge lump in her throat.

As she went inside she noticed the incredible silence. "The children were exhausted; they had soup and went to bed. I think they are all asleep already." Gran was still up sitting at the kitchen table, her head in her hands. She came to Beatty and wrapped her in a comforting hug. "Are you alright, dear?" she said.

"I don't want to talk about it Gran, I'm tired and I'm going to bed too."

CHAPTER
TWENTY

Shimmering Mirage

Weeks passed and no matter how or what she tried, Beatty could not shake the depression and despondency that had descended on her with the news of Robin's probable death. She was exhausted by the years of struggle through the war and now her only lifeline, that Robin would return, meet their beautiful daughter, then they would get married, have a honeymoon in Tasmania and make their own home, was devastatingly severed, she didn't know what to grasp at, there seemed to be no hope. She felt like she was on a Ferris wheel like at Luna Park, the amusement centre which was ever increasing in popularity. Darren had told her it was near Sydney and that he'd like to take her there. The Ferris wheel went round and round and she felt her emotions going round and round and up and down. She felt giddy just thinking about it.

She reflected on her short life and all the misfortune that had befallen her. With dread she realised that the superstition of luck travelling in threes had struck her four times, the loss of the bee business, her parents and now Robin. She dared not think that it would continue. If there was a God, she mused, He is unjust and cruel.

She decided she'd rather make her own way without His misguided involvement just by affirming pure thoughts. She thought how at every turn she seemed to be knocked down. The consequence of Scarlet Fever was missing her exam which meant that she couldn't teach . . . then again, she realised, if she had been teaching she wouldn't have re-established the bees, which now employed four people part-time nor would she have made a correlating discovery in bee fodder and yield, nor written her 'The Seasonal Beekeeper's Journal.'

Intellectually, Beatty knew that Robin wasn't to blame for his capture and consequent lack of survival, but he had promised her that he would return. Internally she swore like a trooper, 'Blooming heck, why did he have to let me down, the bugger!' She couldn't help feeling angry at him whilst still grieving for him and at times feeling resentful . . . she'd waited all these years in vain. This was the biggest disappointment of her life, so far. In quiet moments she compared him to the male bees that played no part in the organisation in the colony, they were merely there to fertilise the eggs. Robin had flown the nest to 'do his bit for his country' and try to assuage his guilt about the bee loss and in doing so he had abandoned Beatty and his egg, who he'd never met, never even known about, for life. Sure, she felt resentful, who wouldn't?

She was paralysed by de-motivation and despondency. Amelia had completely taken over the library job, Beatty was disinterested. Bob, Eddie and Harry were keeping an eye on the bee business. The three of them looked quite a sight, a gangly boy not quite a man, a man on crutches and a man without an arm. Beatty had bought a bee trolley and organised a ramp and this made it possible for them to manage all aspects of the business. They worked within their capacity but missed Beatty's driving determination and organisational skills. Before finding out about Robin, Beatty had stayed up late at night writing letters of explanation to all their old stockists and renewing suppliers. Reply letters were pouring in and Gran not knowing what to do with them handed the whole bundle to Eddie. Everyone in the household tried to fill in for Beatty's slackness, yet it became apparent to all that the house wasn't as clean, the meals weren't as delicious, nothing was the same, and everything had again lost its lustre.

Beatty overheard a conversation on the other side of the blanket between Gran and Amelia early one morning as Amelia prepared to go to the library. "But, Gran, can't Beatty at least take over the afternoon shift at the library?"

"Well I suppose. In fact it could do her the world of good, it did before. She used hard work as a panacea for your parents' deaths. Leave it to me; I'll have a word with her."

Thankfully with the warmer weather and her arthritis in remission, Gran was able to be up and about and doing more, picking up the slack where Beatty simply couldn't be bothered.

Sitting around the breakfast table, Gran decided to have a serious talk with Beatty. "Now, listen to me, dear, it has been months since we heard about Robin. It's time you got over him. Amelia wants you to take over the afternoon shift again. We all want you back, Beatty. The little ones especially need you, think of them. You should go out with Eddie, he has been an amazing support or even with that Darren, who is constantly dropping off flowers and chocolates for you, he's keen. It isn't healthy to mope around for so long. We're all sick and tired of it, dear. You've got to shake it. I won't have it any longer."

"Gosh, Gran, I can't help how I feel."

"That's not true, dear. What about all your positive thoughts that you used to espouse? What about your saying that everything will be brighter in the morning light?"

"They don't work, I was positive Robin would come home but he didn't."

"Well, I think I noticed that they did work, when you were using them. But now, you are being selfish, wallowing in self pity, dear. Please make an effort for those that love you."

"Ok, Gran. Finished with the lecture?"

"How about we do a thorough spring clean, today, to have a fresh start before the festive season? That always makes one feel better."

"Ok, I suppose." Beatty wearily replied cradling her tea cup in her hand, abandoning her porridge due to sudden extreme loss of appetite. She helped to clear away the table. She took the little girls through to the laundry/washhouse to clean them up, dressed them in their best, bundled them into the cab of the truck and drove to Mavis and Bob's place.

On the way over she searched the faces of the men in uniform walking along. She always continued to search the crowds for her beloved's face. There were a lot more soldiers returning now and her obsession increased.

"Anyone home?" She called as she knocked on the door, pushing it open. Mavis came along the corridor.

"Hi, Mavis, does it suit you to have the girls for the day?"

"Sure, Bob and I don't have anything particular planned. You know, you really ought to think about getting the phone on then it would be so much easier for you to just ring us. We said we'd be happy to baby-sit, the girls are no trouble, they just help me do whatever cooking or gardening I was doing anyway and I just have a bit more mess to clean up."

"I have to do the library this afternoon; Amelia is getting antsy n Gran n I are going to spring clean today. So, I'll pick the girls up on my way home from work. Ok?"

"Sure, and you know if ever you want time to relax or to go out for fun, we could have them stay overnight."

"Thanks, but that is not very likely." Beatty bobbed down and hugged each girls, giving Jenny an extra squeeze-y hug and said, "You be good girls, help out Nanny and Pop and do what they say."

"We will, Mummy," they choroused.

Gran had already started when Beatty got back, her hair tied up in a check scarf. She was singing to herself, looked up and said, "Look dear, Darren called by with flowers and chocolates, again, it's his birthday soon and he would like the pleasure of your company. I think you ought to go, it would do you good to have something to look forward to."

Beatty tied a scarf around her head, too then grabbed a duster and started up high removing cobwebs. She then took the rugs out to the line and beat them. Great clouds of dust billowed up and sent Beatty into a coughing fit which brought the attention of Eddie who came over and offered to do the nasty job. Beatty accepted.

She went in, scrunched up and wet some newspaper and cleaned the windows, scrubbing off dust and fly poops. Before she knew it she was feeling uplifted and was humming to herself. Nearby, Gran was sweeping and humming too. Really there is nothing like a good clean to shift negative energy and with clean windows everything will definitely look brighter in the morning light!!! Beatty started to tell herself positive affirmations.

Gran and Beatty sat at the table for a quick late lunch of bread and honey and a cup of tea. They enjoyed an easier amicability and the tranquility of the house. A sense of satisfaction was creeping in. Gran hoped this would be a turning point for Beatty.

After their repast, Beatty filled a bucket with hot soapy water and scrubbed the floor throughout the house, when she went outside to empty the mop bucket she sat on the little stone wall by the outhouse, enjoying the sun on her exhausted body. The sun scorched swirling fiery colours through her eyelids. She watched the psychedelic display and she became mesmerised. Before she knew it the sun had lulled her to sleep.

She recognises herself and watches as she glides along the shimmering desert sands, she is swelteringly hot, weighted down by the nun's habit that she wears, she carries a large upturned tortoise shell which she's filled with phallic shaped cacti which are wilting in the sun, and under them is honeycomb with young larvae preserved in each prism. She felts hot, exhausted, thirsty and hungry. In the distance she spots Robin, he is resting at the base of a date palm; he looks thin but happy to see her. As she approaches he disappears into a shimmering mirage in the heat.

Suddenly Beatty woke, beads of sweat had formed on her brow and rivulets of sweat ran down her dress. She was startled by the dream which had a nightmare quality. She jumped up with the realisation that she was late for work at the library. As she dashed through the house her eyes fell on the photograph of the family, which she had framed, with Robin in it, it was super dusty from the stirred up dust, so in a brief indulgence of sentimentality she ran her sleeve over it to dust it off. Overcome by melancholy and in her haste she dropped it, it shattered to the floor, Gran rushed in with the sound of the smashing glass, Beatty had already bobbed down to pick up the pieces, "Don't fret dear, you go, I'll clean it up, otherwise you'll be late." But a splinter had lodged itself in her finger and as she withdrew it, her blood flowed. She wrapped it in a hankie. Beatty then cranked the truck and zoomed off, a vague state of mind possessed her.

She parked the truck around the back, ran down the lane and dashed up the stairs, bumping into a patron. "I'm so sorry," she said.

"Beatty, you're just the person I was hoping to bump into," it was Darren, "did you get the flowers and chocolates?"

"Yes, I did, thank you, the flowers are beautiful and the children always get excited for chockies."

"Will you come to dinner with me for my birthday on Sunday night?"

She was about to decline then thought of Gran's words of wisdom and how the children deserved for her to make an effort and be happy, so she replied, "Yes, thank you, that would be lovely."

She'd be very late for work now, Mrs. Richardson would be cross.

CHAPTER
TWENTY-ONE

Bee Comes U

Beatty was breathless as she swung open the heavy wooden door into the library, Mrs. Richardson's face was pinched and severe as she was about to chastise Beatty for her tardiness but on seeing her flushed face instead said, "Welcome back, Beatty, I've missed you, Amelia is lovely but she isn't anywhere near as particular as you are. Come let's have a cup of tea together and you can catch your breath then tell me all about how you are getting on. How are those beautiful little girls of yours?"

They sat and chatted and Beatty divulged more than she'd intended to. She really didn't have many people or opportunities to confide her troubles to. Gran was too brusque, Mavis was grieving too and Kabbarli was a very sporadic visitor, and Mrs. Parker next door, well, she was the president of the bush telegraph communications committee! She told of her shock to the news of Robin and her subsequent depression and despondency.

"Perhaps you have a late bout of 'baby blues'?" Mrs. Richardson suggested trying to be understanding.

"Well, it would have to be extraordinarily late, Jenny is already two." Beatty replied.

"Wow, my goodness, is she really? My, how time flies. It can't be that then, must be something else troubling you."

"No, I know what it is, it's about Robin. I loved him and pinned too much hope on his homecoming. It's like all my future dreams are dashed. But good news about the bees, we are actually making a very good profit now. I have some money to put down as a deposit for land and we are at long last going to have our own flushing lavatory."

"Well, there you are. You have lots of positive plans for the future. Well done for turning the situation around. Your parents would have been mighty proud of you, Beatrice," Mrs. Richardson stood up, gave her a quick hug and said, "I best go and prepare dinner for my crowd, they do so much more now they are getting older but they still like their mummy's cooking."

"Did your husband return well from the war?" Beatty asked.

"He did, but a few days later I told the drunken slob we didn't want to carry his load and to go and find lodgings elsewhere."

"Wow that was mighty strong of you." Beatty replied feeling flabbergasted.

"Well, I know myself so well now. The children and I have a good routine that we don't need the likes of him spoiling our lives. Best go, good to catch up with you."

Beatty walked into the cleaning closet, she absentmindedly fingered her locket. She smiled at her memories of her secret rendezvous with Robin, it was only the second time they had made love but it was also, sadly, the last. She grabbed the cloths and started to work. Her mind meandered to Darren, he was charming, he liked the high life and to treat her to gifts and dinner, he did excite her. He wasn't Robin, there would always be a special place in her heart for Robin, her first love, her beloved, but it could be fun to spend some time with Darren and see where it lead. Given time she was sure she could fall in love with him. She was weary from the day of spring cleaning and she hoped that her work was adequate to meet Mrs. Richardson's high expectations and exacting standards.

She finished up and drove like an automaton to collect the girls from Mavis and Bobs.

She knocked and the girls almost bowled her over when they greeted her. They had done lots of things and were filled with excitement about their day, they all chatted at once. Mavis had put the decorated biscuits they'd made into a tin for them to take home and Bob had made matchstick houses with them.

"Look at mine, Mummy," said Jenny holding out her chubby and grubby hand, "Pop says it looks like a dunny about to fall down, I'm gonna give it to Harry for his birthday."

"That is very good, sweetie." Beatty said distractedly.

As they were leaving Beatty remembered she had a question, "Mavis, funnily enough, I do have a dinner invite for Sunday, can you look after the girls?"

"We'd love too, they can stay the night. Drop them here in the early arvo."

Beatty grabbed their gear and bundled the girls into the truck. They were weary, too, having missed their naps in their eagerness to participate in the busy household activities. Usually they were really good cooperative children but they started whingeing and Beatty felt agitated.

She looked down at the three little girls sitting on the bench seat, Evie by the door, Mary next and Jenny slightly forward and askew, a little set of steps all squeezed in. As they approached an intersection, Beatty was studying the face of a soldier on the corner; a melancholic wave washed over her and took away her concentration. She proceeded through the crossroads without giving way, suddenly out the corner of her eye she saw a car appear on her right, she swerved, tyres squealing, slammed on the brakes and hit the curb, narrowly avoiding a serious accident but abruptly throwing Jenny into the dashboard, and she crumpled in an unconscious heap. Evie and Mary had just slid off their seats. Beatty panicked, "Jenny, baby, are you ok?" She slapped her face, gently. Jenny didn't wake, she had a gash on her temple and blood was pouring profusely from it. The soldier came over and offered assistance in the form of a handkerchief. Beatty got Evie to cradle Jenny and Mary to hold the cloth to her forehead. She drove the short distance home carefully, dropped the older girls off, and ordered a wet cloth and Amelia to accompany her to hold Jenny to the hospital. As they drove along Beatty constantly reassured and sang to Jenny in a wavering voice.

They waited to be treated. Beatty rocked back and forth with Jenny, both to comfort her and to hide the fact they she was in fact shaking like a eucalyptus leaf in a cyclone. Guilty thoughts overwhelmed her mind like a tempest. She made a promise to 'what-ever' that if Jenny could only pull through she would be a better mother and make more of an effort to break out of her limbo land state of despondency. They got called in. Jenny was tended to. The doctor gave Beatty a hard time about the accident. Jenny needed eight stitches, as the doctor finished she stirred and said, "Mummy?"

"Yes, darling, Mummy's here." Beatty whispered back, tears in her eyes, relief flooding in as Jenny regained consciousness. The doctor explained that Jenny had a mild concussion and would need to stay in hospital overnight under observation. Beatty held her in her arms all night. Amelia was slumped in a chair nearby, fast asleep. Beatty made one resolve after another, trying to turn her life around. Gran was right she had to do it for the children. Her depression was self indulgent, she had to shake it. She felt sure that the emotions she'd felt for Jenny when she was unconscious were enough to shake her out of her closed shell forever. The doctor suggested that she consider getting a safer car for the family, than a truck, one with a back seat for children. She said she would seriously consider it. Despite a lack of sleep, on the drive home Beatty felt she was in a state of hyper-alertness, 'Good,' she thought, 'that close call has knocked the lethargy out of me.'

She laid Jenny in her bed then she went into the washroom, she tip-toed up to see her reflection in the mirror, her face was flushed, she remembered that she was sunburnt from falling asleep in the sun yesterday. Was that only yesterday? It felt like ages ago. She studied her face, she was sure that she had aged overnight. She ran her finger around in her all purpose cream and instantly she thought, 'Wow, I could make this to sell.' After a short rest she decided to experiment with making bigger batches of creams.

Her finger throbbed where the piece of glass had cut her. She applied some propolis paste because Kabbarli swore by it saying her people had known of its healing properties for centuries, and had urged Beatty to include it in her skin care range.

Next day, she got in touch with Darren to talk to him about getting a loan to buy a second hand car, "Funny you should ask, I've already talked to my mate, Benny, at the bank and shown him the latest figures and you qualify for quite a substantial loan." It didn't strike Beatty as odd that Darren had done this without her permission, nor did it strike her as odd that he came to pick her up in shiny English racing green MG convertible for their dinner on Sunday evening. Eddie past them on the pavement and whispered low so only Beatty could hear, "I hope you know what you are doing, Bea." Beatty shook her head then threw it back and laughed. Internally she felt uneasy but dismissed the comment as Eddie's jealousy.

Darren drove faster than Beatty felt comfortable and she leant forward to grasp one of the twin humps of the highly French polished walnut veneer dashboard, but it brought back feelings of being out of control and she felt shaky all over again when they arrived for dinner at Beau-jangles Restaurant.

They talked business and she spoke of all the changes she wanted to make. "Well, the business is doing well, but maybe not that well, you'll have to wait for some of those things." Darren explained. Beatty ate very little feeling nervous and self conscious.

She told him of her idea to make healing creams, lip balms and natural skin care from bee products and call her range, 'Bee Comes U', "Wow," he said, "you really are a little go-getter, aren't you?"

"Yes, I suppose and not only that we could make a bee line of confectionary, like honey fudge."

"Great idea, you go for it." He then placed his hand over hers and in a solemn moment said, "I have something for you."

He brought out a velvet covered jewellery box. Beatty opened it apprehensively. There sitting in a bed of silk was a pendant, a honey bee, made of gold filigree, with an opal for the body, rubies for the eyes and diamond chips sparkling in the wings, with a delicate gold chain. "Now you don't have to wear that cheap locket anymore."

"It's beautiful, Darren, thankyou."

"Please, call me 'Ren', all my friends do."

"Thank you Ren." But she didn't put it on and he didn't try to help her.

In the morning Beatty disappeared for a few hours and when she came home she was really excited, "Things are really going to happen around here this afternoon, Gran."

"What's that dear?"

"Well, for starters the telecommunications men will be here to connect a telephone, one is going on in the factory, today, too."

"I don't know how to use those new fangled devices, Beatty."

"Don't worry, Gran, you'll soon learn. Also, we are having a flush lavatory installed."

"Yeah," a chorus of cheers went through the family.

The 'piece de résistance' surprise was a new twin tub washing machine. It felt like Christmas and Beatty was so satisfied that she had made this all happen.

She put a notice up in Andy Brown's corner store asking for a second hand car, including the two new phone numbers. That night she rang Arthur and Elsie to tell them of the good news, they were very happy for her, and happy that they could contact Beatty without having to wait for the mail.

Everyone jumped when the telephone rang, and then crowded around trying to listen in as Beatty talked. This time it was someone in response to the advertisement for a second hand car. "Please tell me about it," said Beatty.

"It's a 1938 Ford Prefect; it has always been a dependable family car. It has induction wipers; it is spacious, tough and reliable. My wife and I don't need anything as big now the youngsters have left home so we thought we would treat ourselves to a new modern convertible to have a fling with freedom and fun for a few years while we are still young enough. If you like you can come for a test drive." It sounded good so Beatty got all the details and asked Eddie to come along to check it out mechanically. The next day they went for a test drive, Beatty was impressed, especially by the inside key ignition and the easy smooth clutch, not like the challenges in the truck. They went to the bank to organise finance and sealed the deal. Beatty drove the car home and named her; 'Polly' and Eddie drove the truck. When they arrived home the children were so excited they all squeezed in and Beatty drove them around the block.

"I hope you aren't overextending yourself Beatty, all this splurging lately." Gran said with a worried look on her face.

"Don't worry Gran, it'll be fine."

The next day, dressed in her best, her Mother's dress that Gran had altered, Beatty set off to do an advertising run for the 'Bee Comes U' range. She had packed a basket with samples and had hand written in her best copperplate labels on jars neatly packed in boxes on the back seat of the new car. She felt so grown up and important. She walked around the city of Melbourne with her basket, swallowing her nerves to talk to pharmacy and gift shop owners about the new range that she had developed. She was right once she took the lid off her sample jars and the fresh relaxing fragrance of lavender filled the air, everyone was most impressed and Beatty established numerous outlets.

That night she, Amelia and Gran stayed up late making up more creams. Ren suggested to Beatty that he could take her to Sydney to try her luck there and as a treat they could go to Luna Park, but Beatty didn't want to leave the girls for too long so instead she made tiny sample jars up and posted them farther afield to the best stockists of their honey. The telephones rang regularly now with orders for honey and skin care products. All the family apart from the three little girls had a role to play in the revived business. They were running one hundred and twenty hives at Greendale and product enhancing, it was a huge achievement.

The phone rang one evening, everyone crowded around as usual as Beatty answered it, and it was Ren. "Scoot, you lot," Beatty waved her hand at them.

"Listen, Beatty, I was thinking we could go to church together in the morning."

"No thanks, Ren, I don't think so. My days of kneeling and statues and incense are a thing of the past. I used to believe but I was shunned in the most un-Christian way. I believe in inner strength and the power of positive thinking. No way do I go to church anymore."

"Oh," Ren was stunned speechless; he hadn't seen this side of Beatty before, "well then, how about dinner next weekend?"

"Sure, we'll talk closer to the time."

Beatty went to bed weary but with a deep sense of satisfaction. She passed her rosary beads through her fingers with her new mantra, 'Love, Peace, Inner Strength, Harmony, Joy . . .' The words circled her brain as she fell asleep.

The day dawned warm and sunny and Beatty decided that they were going on a daytrip to Arthur and Elsie's, a way to take everyone for a treat and christen the 'new' second-hand car, she rang to check that it would be ok and as usual, Arthur was most amenable. She knocked next door and Eddie said he was up for a trip to the country, he would drive the truck with Amelia and Harry, Beatty would drive the car with Gran in the front with Gregory in the middle, and Rupert and the three girls lined up in the back. A full picnic hamper groaned in the trunk at the rear. It was a long drive and they played travelling games and sang songs to help pass the time.

When they arrived Arthur and Elsie were impressed but overwhelmed by Beatty's tribe. Beatty's tribe ran wild in the open pastures filling their lungs with the fresh highland air; the boys practiced yodeling like a kookaburra. All the fellows including Arthur played paddock cricket, amidst whoops and squeals. Elsie had baked up a storm after the telephone call; she'd made scones and a spicy apple tea cake. The veranda had an odd assortment of wicker chairs pulled up and the boys sat on the steps of the farm house in the shade, flushed from their exertion. On the many different occasions that Beatty had visited, sometimes with one of the boys she'd talked to the kind older couple about her family and all her responsibilities but it wasn't until they saw them all in one place that the realisation of Beatty's achievements hit them. They were most impressed and their estimation of Beatty went up tremendously.

They walked about the property, exploring old barns and checking out the extraction room and the beekeeping supplies. Arthur liked Eddie, finding him an affable, decent fellow, impressed by his willing cooperative spirit and no trace of a 'poor me' victim mentality, despite his missing arm. He asked intelligent questions and was genuinely interested in how Arthur had increased his business. Before they left, Arthur pulled Beatty aside and said, "I know how much you like it here so I thought I'd let you know that Else and I are going to subdivide and sell up some of the property, thought we'd give you first option. We'll keep one hundred acres but the rest will be in fifty acre lots. We'd like you to have the one with the cottage and apricot orchard. You could have your own bees on your own property, just like you have always wanted. Of course you'll have to talk to the bank and organise your finance, but we'll do you a good deal. Let me know."

"Oh, Arthur," Beatty threw her arms around him in her excitement, "of course I'd love to."

The country air had lulled everyone to sleep, including Gran, and Beatty daydreamed about her own little place in Goulburn Valley as she drove home. Her car load was weary and ready for bed when they arrived home, in direct contrast to the truck's occupants who were lively, chatting away, especially Amelia who seemed to have an extra sparkle in her eyes.

Beatty was so excited that night she could barely contain herself so she rang Ren to tell him the wonderful news. "It's what I've always wanted, and Father talked about having the bees on their own land, too. It's a lovely spot, the cottage is small and needs a bit of renovating but it is so beautiful. The orchard is well established and it's in full productivity. Just wait til you see it Ren!"

"Hold your horses, Beatrice May, you've already spent so much lately, it would be unwise to commit to more."

"Oh, Ren, don't be a spoilsport, this is my dream, and besides its a prudent business decision."

"I'm just warning you."

"I'll go to the bank tomorrow; surely Benny will see how well the business is doing." Beatty said.

"I don't think that is wise; why not wait for a while, til the next summer's harvest?" Ren advised.

Beatty was puzzled why Ren wasn't encouraging her, she shook her head but she realised he hadn't burst her bubble and she went to bed still filled with anticipation.

When she woke she had an inspired plan and she started to organise her day accordingly. The children needed feeding, and then she would clean herself and get dressed up in one of Mother's matching twin set suits. It was a soft woollen fabric in pale egg shell blue, hardly worn and suited Beatty perfectly. She tucked her locket under her blouse and borrowed a string of pearls from Mrs. Parker. She used a light touch of Gran's lipstick. She paraded in front of the family and had an assortment of comments, mainly positive about being grown up and beautiful. She was ready.

As she entered the bank, nerves fluttered in her stomach, she felt it was such a huge step to take. Benny was welcoming and Beatty put her proposal to him.

He leant back in his chair, buttons straining on his jacket, he looked her up and down and she felt somewhat uncomfortable.

"My records show you've spent all your savings within a few weeks, you have no deposit and already a substantial loan. It would be irresponsible of us to lend you anymore at this stage. Why don't you wait til the end of season when you fill some big orders and get lots of cheques?"

Beatty couldn't understand why people seemed hell bent on obstructing her ultimate dream. If she waited, would another opportunity as good as this ever present itself? She thought not.

"Forget it for now, I'm not waiting, I'll find another way."

Benny started back-pedalling, "Let me know what you decide, how we can help you. We don't want to lose your custom at this bank."

"No doubt Ren will tell you."

Beatty slumped at the kitchen table. Gran was worried; she hated to see her on this emotional rollercoaster ride. Gran bustled about making tea, then sat down and suggested they try to figure out a way to make it happen.

"We could put this house up as security, what do you think?" Gran said.

"Oh, no, I wouldn't want to do that."

"Why don't you talk to Ren, he's the one with the accounting degree?"

"Yes, I'll ring him later."

Just as Beatty was getting ready for her library job, Eddie called out at the back door, "How about I take the girls for a walk, anyone up for it?" Amelia put cardigans on the three little girls and on herself and they set off for their afternoon stroll. Beatty didn't like to be missing out. At times she felt resentful of her workload.

After work, Gran had made a special meal and Amelia and Harry insisted on washing up. Beatty picked up 'A Secret Garden,' it was about time she read it to the youngest children, they gathered around her, she read the first two chapters, and then they went to bed most cooperatively. Beatty sat in the armchair trying to puzzle out how she could manage to finance her own place when the phone rang startling her out of her reckoning.

"Hello, Fielding residence." She answered.

"Hello, Beatty?" said the voice, "its Elsie Goldman speaking. It's serious. Arthur's had a stroke; he went by ambulance to the Royal Melbourne Hospital."

CHAPTER
TWENTY-TWO

Jaded Queen Dream

Beatty splashed water on her face grabbed her coat and drove to the hospital. After much persuading, saying she is like a daughter to him and that he has no other family of his own she was allowed in. Arthur looked pale and drawn. Beatty had tears spring to her eyes to see her dear old friend and mentor looking so lifeless. She lightly kissed him on the forehead and sat beside him, holding his hand.

"Is that you, Else?"

"No Arthur. It's me Beatty, how are you feeling?"

"I'm fine, I'll feel better when Else gets here."

Beatty sat beside his bed for a couple of hours until she started nodding off. As she leant down to kiss him 'Good-night' he stirred and said, "How did you go at the bank?"

"Not good, but don't you worry about that now." She replied.

"No, go on tell me . . ."

"Apparently, I've already reached my limit, just with the car. It puzzles me because Darren said that I qualified for a substantial loan. Gran very generously offered that I could use the terrace house, the family home as security, but I don't feel right about that. I'll find a way; I know it's meant to be."

"Yes, I think you are right, it is meant to be yours."

"I better go, Arthur, can I bring you anything, tomorrow?" Beatty asked.

"No, dear, not unless you can bring me my Else and some of her good baking." Beatty chuckled and left the hospital thinking of true love and companionship.

First thing next morning she rang up Elsie to give her the latest news. "He's doing well, but he is pining for you. How about I come up and get you and you stay here for a few days and it will be easy for you to visit him?"

"That would be lovely dear, but I wouldn't want to put you out, you already have so many to look after as it is." Elsie replied.

"Rubbish, Elsie, we'd love to have you stay, wouldn't we Gran?" Beatty called to Gran who was nearby in the kitchen.

"Yes, I suppose, it will be fine." Gran called back.

Beatty prepared for her trip to Goulburn Valley and as she drove she let her mind meander, perhaps she should write a love story based on Arthur and Elsie's life . . .

As she drove down the dusty drive she saw Elsie sitting in a rocking chair on the veranda. She was decked out in her best floral dress, be splendid with hat and even a heavy handed layer of lipstick, her hands were occupied with knitting to keep her from wringing them. She heaved at her case and hobbled down the steps, she didn't think to ask Beatty in, she was ready to go. Beatty hugged her warmly, smelling the freshly baked spicy smell of ginger bread that she had hastily made to take in to Arthur. Their trip was quiet with only sporadic bursts of conversation. Beatty drove straight to the hospital.

Arthur looked much better as Elsie leant her head on him in an embrace. Beatty said she would be back later in the evening. He wove his fingers into her hair in a way which brought them both comfort.

Back at home Beatty cleaned out Harry's room to make it fresh and feminine for Elsie, at present it smelt like stuffy teenage boy's damp clothes and dirty socks. She opened the window to allow some fresh air in, changed the bedding and dusted. She had the help of her three eager little girls under her feet and they all went out to the garden to pick a small posy of fragrant flowers and put them onto the bedside table. When it was time for her to return to collect Elsie, the little children clamoured around her wanting to come but Beatty knew she would have no hope of getting in with her entourage so she quietly slipped out. Arthur was looking remarkably improved from his afternoon infusion of quiet chatting and companionship. Elsie was a helpful house guest and after a simple dinner of soup and bread she insisted on helping clean up the kitchen, then she wearily climbed the stairs and retired for the night.

This became the routine for the next couple of days; Beatty would take Elsie to the hospital after breakfast and collect her before dinner. Each time, in the late afternoon when Beatty visited briefly with Arthur she was amazed at his recovery, so much so that with his rosy, robust health returned he looked out of place in a hospital bed and was told that tomorrow he could go home.

Beatty helped carry Elsie's suitcase out to the car and Elsie hugged everyone who was home. They drove to the hospital with Elsie fidgeting with the edge of her cardigan in her nervous excitement. Arthur was sitting in a chair beside the bed keen to go. He was wearing his usual gear, a white shirt with grey trousers and all held in place with a pair of elasticised braces. Elsie ran her finger inside the braces, straightening the twist, adjusted his shirt collar, dampened her fingers with her own spit and smoothed down his hair where it was tufted from being bed ridden; Arthur patiently succumbed to the pampering. Beatty was reminded of a mother cat grooming her young.

Arthur and Elsie sat in the back seat holding hands on the way home while Beatty thought about her writing, she'd heard back from the Beekeeper's Association that they were interested in her seasonal beekeeping journal and now she longed to write something more fictitious and free. She daydreamed that she could write a love story, but where would she do it and with what time?

At last they were rambling down the rough driveway. Arthur and Elsie insisted that Beatty come in for a cup of tea and something to eat. "That would be lovely but I won't stay long, I need to get back to the children."

She sank into an old armchair feeling quite relaxed and mellow.

"Tell her Arty . . ."

"No, you tell her Else."

"Tell me what?" Beatty asked.

"All right," said Elsie as she pulled up her chair near Beatty. "Arty and I have decided that since we can't take our home and land and bees with us, when we die and seeing as we aren't getting any younger, it could be anytime, and we've decided that we want to give you the cottage and fifty acres."

"Oh," Beatty was speechless. "Oh, that is lovely. But I couldn't."

"We've discussed it and already got it worked out. Arty's nephew is to inherit everything else and we think you are a better custodian of the bees, since you love them and he would only sell up. We've decided you deserve it, you've been a joy to us in our old age, almost like the daughter we never had. So, there, you just have to."

Tears of joy flooded Beatty's eyes, "I don't know what to say, how can I ever express my gratitude?" She hugged then both.

"Come, I'll take you on a tour of the cottage so you know just how much cleaning up you have to do." Elsie rattled a bunch of keys and they walked across the paddock, she continued, "It is many years since we had tenants in the cottage so it is very run down, but I'm sure it will clean up well." Beatty felt she was in a dream as she floated towards her new life.

There was a scattering of dried mud on the narrow veranda from a swallow's nest which had fallen down, knowing of the significance of welcome swallows nests and the subsequent superstition if the nest is damaged she gave an involuntary shiver. Father had always loved swallows and used them as an omen and could even predict the weather and seasons by their movements. The cottage was small and damp and the smell of mildew overwhelmed her nostrils as she entered. Sure, it was run down but with some tender loving care she would have it homely in next to no time. There was some dilapidated furniture, a few simple wooden beds and a solid black-wood table and chairs. Rodents had left their calling cards on the benches in the kitchen and she could hear a scampering in the walls. Beatty could barely contain her joy and enthusiasm at the prospect of getting this place liveable. Energy surged through her, 'nothing like a new project to give me a new lease on life' she thought.

She hugged them both 'good-bye' and planned her fresh start while driving home. 'The little girls and Harry should come and live with me, while Gran stays with the twins and Amelia so they can continue their schooling. The twins can take over Harry's newspaper and delivery job and he can work the bees full time and Amelia can do the library job on her own as well as school. I'll scrub the walls and floor, then paint and make inside fresh, we'll move in then the fellows can do the outside, later on.' By the time she arrived home she had it all worked out. She was sure she would miss the ease with which she could leave the little ones with Gran, still they were growing up and she'd be able to get them involved with the business and farm life.

Gran was the only one still up and she hugged Beatty with joy at the news of her good fortune. They sat up making plans and Beatty could barely sleep she was so filled with excitement.

In the morning she sang as she prepared breakfast and announced to all the family who were tremendously happy, all except the twins who wanted to join in the new adventure. "It isn't fair," they complained, "why do we have to stay behind and go to school and miss out on all the fun?"

"Because you need an education to put you in good stead for the rest of your life, that's why. No argument and no discussion will be entered into!" Said Gran in a no nonsense tone. Amelia was overjoyed that she was staying, the prospect of country life and hard work didn't appeal to her anyway.

Beatty went next door to tell Eddie who was jubilant and offered assistance with the move. Then she rang Darren who was very pleased and asked what the value of the property was worth.

"Oh, Ren, you know I don't ask those sorts of questions. It is worth the world to me, I just love it."

Beatty packed up a cleaning supply kit and made enquiries about paint prices. She and Harry went ahead to clean up and paint and prepare the cottage. It was the first time she had stayed away overnight from Mary and Jenny and they hung to her and needed cajoling to let her go. Gran promised them to bake a cake and Beatty told them about the excitement of moving to the country but first she had to prepare it. Harry wanted to drive some of the way but Beatty said her nerves weren't up to it at the moment but she promised that in the country she would let him drive the truck around the paddocks.

They worked hard and amicably. Although old and neglected the little cottage was actually very solid and well constructed, it cleaned up beautifully. Towards evening they heard a vehicle pull up.

"I couldn't sit at home and miss out on all the fun of renovating." It was Eddie in the truck. He had brought a collection of timber in the tray as well as some tools to block up mouse holes and fix the veranda. They sat by flickering candle light eating a stew which Beatty had made on the Stanley combustion stove after she had managed to persuade some life into it before she very nearly died of smoke inhalation. It seemed that the flue was blocked by a nest or other assorted debris. Harry said he would climb up and take a look at it tomorrow. They dragged the old mattresses into the dining room and made up make shift beds. As they were dozing off to sleep the fellows told ghost stories until Beatty felt freaked and asked to change the subject to one of renovation plans. They also had a huge job to move the bees from Greendale which would take quite a few nights. Arthur had offered the use of his truck, too, but under strict doctor's instructions to take life easy, he'd be unable to help. They wouldn't attempt to move them during the day ever again. They'd pack them on late afternoon and drive slowly and surely in the dark of night, unloading them before dawn, allowing the bees to do their reconnoitre dances and settle into their new 'paradise pastures', as Beatty had started referring to them.

In less than two weeks of scrubbing and painting and to-ing and fro-ing the cottage was clean and liveable so Beatty packed up her few possessions, Gran sorted spare crockery and bedding, they loaded up and she drove the car while Eddie drove the truck to help out, to their new home, and the promise and start of a new life. She was so filled with anticipation she felt she would burst. The children danced around the house and helped unpack the boxes and set up the things. Eddie got the fire started then hugged them all 'good-bye.' Harry went to see if Arthur needed a helping hand in his workshop. Beatty was at a loss as to what to do with three excited girls so she suggested, "Come on, let's go for an exploration walk," Beatty was hoping to exhaust the girls for the night.

There was a meandering wallaby trail near the creek and they followed it along the ferny banks. They came into a clearing and sat beside a serene pond, listening to the 'bonk' of the banjo frogs, wild ducks paddled on the ponds creating mesmerising ripples on the surface of the water. Dappled sun light cast a magical quality around them. Beatty knew this would become one of her favourite spots to sit and reflect in the entire world. Beatty was lulled into a mediative reverie by the trickling water and frog orchestra. Suddenly, Mary stumbled and called, "Mummy, come quickly, look at what I founded."

Beatty dashed to her, "Are you hurt, sweetie?"

Mary shook her head, "Look!" There before them was a small white cross. The name 'Daisy' was painted on it and had obviously been touched up many times over the years. A clematis vine wrapped around the base of it but had been kept free of the writing.

"Who is it?" Evie asked.

"I don't know . . . Daisy . . . somebody or other; perish the thought, but maybe a pet . . ." Beatty replied. But her curiosity was piqued and she was dying to ask Elsie who it was, but she would have to choose the right time.

A few days later they decided to go for a walk to the clearing again. Beatty placed her precious sweetheart locket around the neck of each story teller and her lavender shawl about their heads; they would play a game of 'raconteur.' The story teller who wore the locket and shawl would have to capture the imaginations of the listeners.

Beatty went first, "There was an old lady who lived deep in the rainforest in harmony with nature. She collected herbs and mosses with healing qualities to supply to the local villagers. Unfortunately, she was losing her sight in her old age. A kind, local girl gave her a puppy as a pet and this dog became her best friend and her eyes. It was the most intelligent dog around; it could help sniff out the herbal medicine to help the villagers. One day the old lady was feeling ill, the dog ran to get help. The villagers gathered around her bed and looked after her until her last breath. Her dog missed her so much that it died shortly after she did. The dog's name was 'Daisy' and she is buried right here. The end."

"Wow, is that a true story, Mummy?" asked Mary.

"No, just make believe, darling, your turn, Evie." Beatty said.

She helped put the locket around Evie's neck and wrapped the shawl around her head.

"Once upon a long, long time ago, there was a fairy queen who lived in this rainforest," she started and looked around for inspiration, "her name was 'Daisy.' She was good and kind and beautiful. One day she kissed a frog, it turned into a banjo and she died of shock and is buried over there. The end." A mischievous grin spread across her face. The two younger girls stories were similar, filled with fairies and magic, fire and sadly, but inevitably, death for Daisy. Beatty would definitely have to ask Elsie about the little grave one day soon.

Days were filled with serene contentment, and only the occasional trip to town to visit their family. At night she went to bed tired but satisfied, the business was more than revived, they are doing well, and her siblings had employment as her Father imagined.

Elsie knocked on the door, "Good morning, I've made you a farmhouse cake, filled with our own eggs, honey and butter."

"Come in Elsie, smells good, thank you. I'm not on good enough terms with the stove to bake, yet. Plus I can't seem to find the time." She gave Elsie a hug, "Come and have a cup of tea with me."

"That would be lovely but I won't stay long. My you have got it cosy in here." She sat as Beatty pottered around, the girls were playing a make believe game under the table.

"Arty is impressed with your research into high yielding bee friendly crops; he said that you are going to plant a field of Lucerne and another of borage."

"Yes, when I first started keeping track of yield, my town bees that I kept as a control had three times as much honey compared to my bush bees so I put it down to not having to fly as far for nectar rich crops. We had a lot of borage in the back yard plus it grew down the sanitary lane behind us. Do you want sugar or honey?" Beatty asked.

"Honey, thanks dear."

Under the table the little girls were sitting in a circle holding hands and chanting a made up ditty, "Daisy, Daisy, Queen of the Fairies, come back from the dead, Daisy, Daisy, kiss the banjo, come and visit us today-O!"

Elsie stirred her tea and blanched when she became aware of what the girls were singing.

"Are you ok, Elsie?" Beatty asked as Elsie dashed outside. She put her arms around her, "I'm sorry did the girls say something to upset you. Is Daisy significant to you, we saw a little cross by the pond."

"Where? Take me there." Silently they walked along the trail to the ferny glade. Elsie knelt down and wept, running her fingers across the writing.

"Who was she, Elsie?" Beatty asked softly.

"My baby girl! Arty must have maintained her cross, I'd even forgotten where it was exactly, I don't come into this eerie place. How did you find it?"

"We followed a little track. We find it serene, we come here to tell stories, and the girls love it here. Tell me about her . . ."

"I was only seven months along when I had pains after doing some heavy lifting and spring cleaning. The doctor told me to rest up, so I did. But as the weeks went by I felt increasingly sick. She had died in utero and I had to have a caesarean section, my womb was so damaged that I had to have a hysterectomy too. That's why we never had children. We had each other, but I guess we both felt something was missing."

"I'm so sorry Elsie, if it is any consolation to you, you have us now." They hugged then wandered back along the track, Beatty was worried the girls would be up to mischief, but they were still playing merrily.

Life was on the up. She was finding quiet reflective time to write in her journal. Ren had visited and had brought fabric for curtains as well as chocolates for the children. He didn't stay long as he had clients to tend to in the city but he promised to visit regularly and asked Beatty out to dinner next time they came to town for a few days. The swallows had returned and started rebuilding their nest. Beatty was happy at last, she loved the quiet and peaceful sounds of nature all around. She woke before the children at dawn and loved to greet the day from the veranda of the cottage, the sun peeking over the verdant, rolling hills and the distant mountains in many shades and hues of purple . . .

Mrs Morton found descriptive passages quite tedious so she skimmed ahead to the next dream.

She is a wet, bedraggled Queen, caught in the rain. Her crown is too big. It slips and she removes it to clean it up. The jewels are dull and there is dust and cobwebs draped around. She cleans and polishes it. She remembers it was once splendid but now it is dull, she knows that with hard work it will regain its shine. She bobs down and removes loaves of bread from an oven, they sink in the middle, and she feels disheartened. All the children come in and gather around, they break the bread and tell her it is delicious even if it did sink in the middle. The rain stops and they gather around the window to look out and see a beautiful rainbow.

CHAPTER
TWENTY-THREE

The Night of the Seventh Dream

Mrs. Morton woke with a mind as crystal clear and sparkling as an autumn ocean on a settled autumn day. She decided she absolutely must speak to her family. She arranged to ring her daughter, "Jennifer, I have to speak to you."

"Ok, Mum, but what's all this about?"

"There are things I have to tell you, and the others. Bring your husband, too. See if everyone can visit this afternoon."

"Ok, Mum, I'll see what I can do; you know how busy everyone is."

"Do you know dear, I fancy some candied honey, clover, I think. Could you bring me some please?"

"Ok, I'll see what I can do. See you about 6pm. Have a good day."

After the phone call, she tried to settle to read, to help her be patient.

Beatty got dressed up for her date with Ren. It had become a fortnightly town event to look forward to. In the country she rarely dressed nicely, she often wore a pair of Father's old overalls for gardening and feeding the animals or the white beekeeping overalls when working with them. She was quite excited at the prospect of having a genuine reason to get dressed up. For the first time that evening she somberly removed the sweetheart locket that Robin had given her. She chose to wear a top with a discreetly revealing décolleté neckline, not another one of Mother's but one she had bought new in the flush of her spending extravagance, the skirt was one of Mother's that Gran had taken in. Nervously she lifted the filigree bee from its box and fastened it around her neck, her hands were shaking and it took a while to do up. Ren arrived with a box of chocolates for the family to share while she was out. As usual he held the door for her and helped her to her seat. They chatted and Beatty told him about the immense joy her family were enjoying with the new car and country lifestyle. Gran and the others were enjoying the modern toilet and when she visited, by merely polishing the new hand basin and brass taps it brought her such satisfaction, knowing she had provided it for them.

He placed his hand over hers and said, "Beatrice May Fielding will you do me the great honour of becoming my wife?" and he slid a little black box with a beautifully simple engagement ring towards her.

Mrs. Morton sat up suddenly, 'I must get dressed up, posh like.' She walked over to her wardrobe and looked through her clothes. So many dresses were missing and the red one in particular she was looking for simply wasn't there, she'd have to have a word with Jennifer. She knew at one stage she had owned lots of beautiful dresses. She found one that suited her mood. A royal blue velvet dress. She tried it on; it was a bit too big and awfully hard to do up the back zip so she left it open and covered the gape with a red cardigan. She wrapped a string of pearls around her withered neck and clipped on opulent looking earrings. She checked her reflection and giggled, 'Oh, isn't this fun,' and she gave a little clap. She couldn't choose between the hot pink lipstick or the magenta so went for hot pink lippy on the top and magenta on the bottom. She put on a hat and pulled it to a jaunty angle while admiring herself in the mirror. With her worn sheepskin slippers on her feet she shuffled along the corridor to visit her friends.

She needed a priest too, today. She accosted the next best thing, a plump Salvo lady doing her rounds with magazine and tea trolley. She pulled her into a corner of the day room, competing with the TV to confess and ask for absolution of her sins. The Salvo lady nodded to show she was listening but was highly confused by this adorable old lady confessing to attempted murder.

The sweet old man, Edward tried to whistle her as she past and told her she was looking exceptionally beautiful. She restlessly paced the hall waiting for her family. She knew she couldn't sleep; she couldn't afford to lose her clarity. She decided she would pack up her things to be ready for when her family arrived.

She fingered her precious things, a tarnished locket with worn engraving on the back from worry stone rubbing, a big blue tom bowler marble with a chip out of it, a cobalt blue eye bath and some worn out poems and letters . . . she looked at her hands in amazement, when did her knuckles get so swollen and the skin so crêpe and covered in sun spots? She ran her hands over the frayed patches of silk in her quilt. Inside she still felt that she was a young teenager but age had crept in and her body betrayed her.

Jennifer and her husband arrived, in the corridor before she entered she asked the nurse, "How is she this evening?"

"She's well, been up all day, amazingly lucid, but taking it hard, she wants out. We'll give her a sedative for the night after your visit."

"Hello, Mum, what are you doing?"

"I'm packing up to come home, of course. If the others won't come to visit me I'll go to visit them."

"The others will come on the weekend, Mummy, just relax, sit down, let's chat. Here's your honey. You remember my husband, Adam."

"Of course I do, dear." He leant forward to give her a perfunctory hug.

"What's up in the world of bees, Adam?" Mrs. Morton asked eating honey from the jar with a mother of pearl spoon.

"Actually, it's terrible news. There is Veroa mite on our doorstep in New Zealand. Australia is the only country free of this pest. Do you realise the implications of this?" Adam asked.

"Of course I do, if we lose our bees then the whole world will starve within years. No bees, no pollination, no fertilisation, no food, eventually no people. So what's Australia doing about it?"

"Last I heard Australia is shipping out lots of Bees to help pollinate orchards and crops, to countries like America and Europe."

"But what I mean is," said Mrs. Morton trying not to be impatient, "is what is Australia doing to protect herself from bio-attack?"

Adam raised his eyebrows, he hadn't seen his wife's Mum ever this on the ball since she was admitted here. "There is an Australian scientist, a Dr Anderson who is developing a protective serum."

"Oh good," she said and turning towards Jennifer says, "What I wanted to say is that I love you, always have and always will and the others, of course. I am disappointed in them but I have always done my best for them, for all of you. You do understand, don't you?"

"Yes, of course, Mummy."

"Now I have to tell you the story behind 'Seeds of Suspicion'.

Just then Nurse Kristy bustled in.

"I thought you were meant to be taking some time off." Mrs. Morton said.

"Yes, I am, this evening is my last shift, I get a week of leave then I'm transferred to the other section for a while. That stupid Laura dobbed on me, I was only playing a prank on her. Still some people can't take a joke. I suppose." She was so busy tidying up that when she looked at Mrs. Morton she got a shock to see her. "My, you're a silly old chook for getting yourself in such a ridiculous outfit. Such a waste of time and energy," she said condescendingly. She grabbed a flannel and washed off the lipstick.

"Can't you wait until my guests go, before degrading me?" Mrs. Morton asks.

"No, this won't take long." She roughly pulled the dress over her head and slipped her nightie on.

Mrs. Morton was flushed and annoyed, "Where was I?"

She looked blank as the fugue fog started to descend, "Oh, that's right," she said her face brightening up, "I must tell you about 'Seeds of Suspicion . . .'" Adam was restless in his seat and cleared his throat and Jennifer said, "Mother, we must dash, Adam has a meeting and we have the grandkids coming for dinner, can we talk about that next time?"

"But Jen, I must tell you. You are the only one who would understand. You are my precious Jenny wren; you were the joy of my life." Jennifer's eyes were moist as she kissed her Mother 'Good-bye' on the cheek.

Mrs. Morton wandered down the corridor to say 'Goodnight' to the moon. She tried the courtyard door but couldn't open it, it was locked tight. Nurse Laura came along and looped her arm through hers and said so long as they weren't too long, she'd accompany her.

The twilight sky was like a faded velvet curtain, the clouds parted and a shaft of moonlight formed an eerie path to the heavens. A ring of water droplets encircled the moon like a celestial halo.

Mrs. Morton whispered, "Thank you, dear moon for your comforting light, good night."

Laura said, "Knowing you has enriched my life, I feel so much more positive and closer to the things that really matter since I met you," as they wandered back to her room.

Laura brought her pills and a cup of tea and settled her down for the night.

She picks up the book, yet she feels so drowsy she might just skip ahead to the seventh dream, but the book grows heavy, her eyes close, try as she might she couldn't keep them open any longer. The light in the room shimmers and dances, her head spins. The book slips down the coverlet and with a soft thud falls to the floor, she carefully pushes back the bedding and places her bare feet on the cold tiles, everything falls away and she is young again. *She flies across a lush meadow into her beloved Robin's arms. He enfolds her like a golden cape of love and whispers in her ear, "I've been waiting for you, Honey Bea, I've searched every face that comes through here, longing for only yours." She notices she has shiny red shoes on her feet. In his bronzed hand he carries an ornate brass key. She turns to kiss her daughter on her forehead and cheeks, leaving behind a collection of swirling lipstick mandalas. She turns back to Robin and with arms around each other they glide over an ethereal rainbow and slide down into a spa bath of golden bubbling honey. Flowers float on the surface as if they were infused in an intoxicating punch.*

Now, all that separated her from her true love was a breath or a heartbeat away.

Dear Reader,

The words within the book lay dormant, lying in wait for the next person to read a new breath of life into them. Quite unexpectedly, an exquisite breath was drawn in, with the heavy fragrance of honeysuckle, the flower of past longings and dreams. Your consciousness altered and the air around you became electric as if filled with a swarm of bees . . . You started to read, drawing exquisite life into the words upon the page. I give thanks for the breath of life, yours and mine.